xoxo, **Betty** *and* **Veronica**

Liv

by Christa Roberts

Grosset & Dunlap
An Imprint of Penguin Group (USA) Inc.

GROSSET & DUNLAP
Published by the Penguin Group
Penguin Group (USA) Inc., 375 Hudson Street,
New York, New York 10014, USA
Penguin Group (Canada), 90 Eglinton Avenue East, Suite 700,
Toronto, Ontario M4P 2Y3, Canada (a division of Pearson Penguin Canada Inc.)
Penguin Books Ltd., 80 Strand, London WC2R 0RL, England
Penguin Group Ireland, 25 St. Stephen's Green, Dublin 2,
Ireland (a division of Penguin Books Ltd.)
Penguin Group (Australia), 250 Camberwell Road, Camberwell,
Victoria 3124, Australia (a division of Pearson Australia Group Pty. Ltd.)
Penguin Books India Pvt. Ltd., 11 Community Centre,
Panchsheel Park, New Delhi—110 017, India
Penguin Group (NZ), 67 Apollo Drive, Rosedale, Auckland 0632,
New Zealand (a division of Pearson New Zealand Ltd.)
Penguin Books (South Africa) (Pty.) Ltd., 24 Sturdee Avenue,
Rosebank, Johannesburg 2196, South Africa

Penguin Books Ltd., Registered Offices: 80 Strand,
London WC2R 0RL, England

Published by Grosset & Dunlap, a division of Penguin Young Readers Group,
345 Hudson Street, New York, New York 10014. GROSSET & DUNLAP is a
trademark of Penguin Group (USA) Inc. Printed in the U.S.A.

ISBN 978-0-448-45578-5   10 9 8 7 6 5 4 3 2 1

"I've been dreaming about this for months," Veronica Lodge said happily. She pushed her expensive wraparound sunglasses on top of her head and smiled over at Betty. "Haven't *you?*"

"You've been dreaming about walking around the mall?" her best friend, Betty Cooper, teased. The two girls were spending the first official day of summer vacation together at the outdoor Riverdale Mall.

Veronica had already bought three new bathing suits and a new pair of sandals. Betty had picked up some peace sign earrings and a pretty purple tank top that would be great for the hot days ahead.

Betty pointed to a vitamin store across the way. "Or were your dreams filled with triple protein shakes?"

Veronica nudged her in the ribs with her elbow. "You're *so* funny, Betty. What I *meant* was that I've been wishing for it to just be summer already for the past three months." She sighed. "And now it is! I want this to be the best summer of our lives. Days at the beach with all our friends, summer concerts with The Archies, bike rides, tons of movies, shopping till we drop. I want to do all the things that we don't have time for the rest of the year."

Betty nodded. She felt the same way Veronica did. *No pressure, no rules, no homework* . . . she thought wistfully as they walked by a large fountain where some little kids were splashing one another and giggling in the summer sun.

To Betty's surprise, Veronica slipped off her purple flip-flops and, holding them in her hand, hopped up on the low marble ledge that surrounded the fountain.

"If we want to dip our toes in, who's to stop us?" Veronica asked.

"Um, that security guard?" Betty whispered as a frowning, mustached guy in a security uniform looked over at them.

"Oh, sorry," Veronica called over to the man, winking. "It's not like I'm going to swim laps or anything." She slipped her flip-flops back on. "Betty, I'm in serious need of a mani-pedi, and there's a new salon that opened here last month. What's the name of that place again?" She thought for a second, then snapped her fingers. "Beauty Town. What do you say . . . do you have time for some best friend bonding? We can both get manicures and pedicures. We could even get organic seaweed facials!"

Betty hesitated. She looked down at her nails. The red polish she'd put on last week was chipped and flaking. A manicure would be a cool way to spend the afternoon. And Beauty Town was really nice . . . they even mixed custom nail polish colors for you. Not that Betty had been there yet—but she'd heard all about it at school.

Then she took a look inside her wristlet. After buying the earrings and tank top, she and Veronica had stopped for soft pretzels and lemonade, which left her with exactly eight dollars and thirty cents.

"Well . . . ," Betty started. Getting her nails done would be nice . . . but all that niceness cost money. And an organic facial was out of the question.

Veronica took Betty's arm and steered her in the direction of Beauty Town. "I'm thinking metallic. Maybe something with a purple sheen to it . . ."

Betty held back. "That sounds cool, Ronnie, and I love a good spa day just as much as the next girl in Riverdale, but Beauty Town is kind of expensive, and I'm trying to save my money this summer."

"Save?" Veronica repeated, looking confused. "For what?"

Betty sighed. "Remember how my laptop

died last month? Well, I need to get a new one, and my parents said they can't afford to buy me one right now. Either I have to wait until later this fall—or I have to pay for it myself."

"That's going to take an awful lot of babysitting, Betty," Veronica said, wrinkling her nose. "Laptops aren't exactly cheap."

"Yeah, I've heard," Betty said wryly. "That's why I have to get a real job this summer. I can't just sit home and hope people call me to babysit. I really can't spend money I don't have on a manicure—let alone a pedicure or a facial."

Betty knew that Veronica had never worried about money in her life. And why would she? After all, Veronica's father, Hiram Lodge, was an übersuccessful businessman. The Lodges were one of the richest families in the country. The idea of Veronica worrying about how to pay for a manicure—well, it just wouldn't happen.

Veronica shrugged as they slowly walked

past Beauty Town. "I get where you're coming from, but don't forget, summer is just beginning." She waved to one of the nail technicians inside the salon. "You have *plenty* of time to find a real job."

Betty wasn't convinced. "You have no idea how hard it is to get a job, Ronnie. And I'm not talking about my dream job, either. I'm talking about *any* job. There's so much competition!"

Veronica dismissively waved her hand around as if the idea of competition was the silliest thing she'd ever heard of. "Betty, you're the most amazing, dedicated, and hardworking person I know. If anyone can get a job, it's you."

"Tell that to all the places where I filled out applications," Betty told her friend. She had applied for at least a dozen jobs before school let out, but other than one interview for a receptionist job at a car dealership—which she didn't get—she hadn't had one bite of interest.

"What if no one hires me?" Betty said,

feeling glum. She held up her hand and began to tick off her worries on her nonmanicured fingers. "Firstly, summer is not as long as you think. Secondly, all the good jobs go fast. Thirdly, everyone knows that work experience looks good on your college applications, which makes it twice as hard to find one. No, I take that back—ten times as hard," she said, dejected. "Fourthly, I really, really need a new laptop!"

But as Betty finished, she realized that Veronica wasn't really paying attention. Instead, her blue eyes were trailing after a couple of trendy-looking girls carrying bright pink shopping bags.

Belle Pink. Betty recognized the logo and signature color of Veronica's favorite new store at the mall.

Veronica squeezed Betty's arm, making her wince.

"You have totally just inspired me, Betty. You know how I've been thinking about a career in fashion, right?" Betty opened her mouth to reply, but Veronica kept going.

"Well, a job at Belle Pink is the perfect place to start!"

Betty was pretty sure that *Veronica* and *job* had never been used in the same sentence before now. In fact, it almost made her burst out laughing.

But Veronica looked dead serious. Before Betty knew what was happening, Veronica marched them into the store. French music was blasting from speakers in the shape of the Eiffel Tower. Customers were browsing chrome clothing racks of superchic tops, pants, and dresses.

Betty coughed. "What's that smell?" It smelled like lilies—a field of them.

"That's Belle Pink's signature scent, Femme Fatale. They spray all their clothes with it."

"What happens when you have to throw something in the wash?" Betty asked, only half joking.

"They sell Femme Fatale laundry detergent, too," Veronica explained as if that should have been obvious.

They made their way past customers and racks of clothes to the back of the store. "*Bonjour.* May I help you?" the sales clerk asked.

Veronica beamed. "*Bonjour, mademoiselle.* May I have a job application, please—I mean, *s'il vous plaît?*"

Betty held back a laugh. Veronica had studied French for years, but her accent was terrible.

"*Merci beaucoup!*" Veronica took a clipboard and began filling out a Belle Pink job application—which, naturally, was pink.

Veronica reached into her oversize purse and pulled out a fistful of colored markers. "See, this is why it's always a good idea to carry supplies with you," she told Betty. Veronica began adding some impromptu fashion sketches and fancy flourishes to the form. "To make it stand out," she whispered.

"Are you sure you want to do that?" Betty asked as Veronica drew a swirl of lime green. "It doesn't look, uh, professional."

Veronica pursed her lips. "But it looks *fashionable*. And that's what's important."

After filling everything in, she handed the clipboard back to the clerk. "Thank you so much. All my contact information is there. So *when* you try to reach me, you can call or text or e-mail. Or all three!"

Betty found it doubtful that Veronica would get a job at Belle Pink. *She has no clue how hard it is,* she thought. *I've applied for tons of jobs, and no one has called me. Veronica thinks she can stroll into her favorite store, snap her fingers, and—presto!—get a job? Get real.*

"Now I know what you're thinking, Betty," Veronica told her as they walked out of the store.

"That we should have gone to the beach?" Betty replied, looking up. The sky was turning a murky shade of gray, and thunder rumbled in the distance. "It's too late now."

Veronica shook her head. "We'll go tomorrow. No biggie. But that's not what I was going to say. I know you think it's stupid for me to get a job."

Betty opened her mouth, but Veronica pressed on. "I've known you for too long, Betty. I know how you think. And you're kind of right. I don't exactly *need* a job. But if I'm going to become a world-famous fashion designer, I need to start somewhere, and it's never too early to get the right kind of experience."

A fat raindrop landed on Betty's head. "Hurry before we get soaked!" she shrieked, sprinting for Veronica's car. "I hope you put the windows up!"

"I'm coming. I'm just checking my messages," Veronica said, tapping on her phone as she jogged to the car. The rain was starting to fall in thick, wet drops. "Belle Pink hasn't called yet."

"Slackers," Betty replied with a smile. The second Veronica unlocked the convertible, Betty dived inside, shivering from the rain.

Veronica was her best friend, and if she

had her heart set on working at Belle Pink, Betty hoped it would happen.

Otherwise? It was going to be a very long summer.

Chapter 2

"Are you ready, boys?" Betty asked, holding a volleyball in her outstretched hand. She swung her bare arm back and easily sent the ball sailing over the net. She and her girlfriends, Midge Klump and Nancy Woods, stood on one side of the beach volleyball net, while Archie Andrews, Reggie Mantle, and Jughead Jones were on the other.

Archie was Betty's on-again, off-again boyfriend. His bright red hair and freckles gave him an all-American look that Betty found endearing, and she loved how polite and well-mannered he was. Being the lead singer and guitarist in his garage band, The Archies, made him even cooler. He was one of the most popular boys at Riverdale High.

The fact that Archie also liked to date Veronica was the part of their relationship that wasn't so cool. He just never seemed to be able to make up his mind which girl he liked better. He was always nice about it, though, and when Betty was with him, she always had fun. So Betty tried not to worry about the future. If she and Archie were meant to be together one day, it would happen.

Betty stayed focused on the ball as Archie passed it to Reggie. Reggie winked over at the girls, then spiked the ball straight into the sand at Midge's feet. "Child's play, ladies."

"Do you guys remember who won the last set we played?" Nancy asked them, her eyes narrowing. Her long dark hair was pulled back in a low ponytail, and she wore a bright green tankini. She picked up the ball and threw it hard across the net. "'Cause I do. And it wasn't you."

"Quit talking and start playing," Jughead called to them, stretching his lanky arms over his head as Archie did an overhand serve.

Jughead was thin, but deceptively strong when he wanted to be.

As the ball came flying toward them, Betty thought Nancy was going to get it. And Nancy thought the same thing about Betty.

"Girls," Midge moaned as the ball plunked to the sand in the space between the two friends. She ran her fingers through her short dark hair, making it stand up. "Someone make a decision, okay?"

Betty dug her toes into the sand. She hated to lose a game of beach volleyball to Archie and the other guys because the boys would never let them forget it. She reached up to adjust the elastic on her blond ponytail and straighten her bright pink sun visor.

"You girls look like you could use a little assistance," Reggie teased. "Veronica! Come help your pals out here."

Betty looked past the volleyball court to where a bikini-clad Veronica lay on her bright blue beach towel next to a sleeping Kevin Keller.

"Yeah, Ronnie. Play with us!" Betty called

out, not because she thought the girls needed help, but because playing a set was always more fun when Veronica was in the mix. But she could tell it was a hopeless cause. Veronica was much too busy to play beach volleyball. What was keeping her occupied was a short stack of fashion magazines and her cell phone.

Veronica looked up from her magazine and gave a little wave. "Sorry. But I can't hold my phone and play volleyball at the same time."

"Couldn't you put your phone down for a little while?" Nancy asked, raising an eyebrow.

Veronica shook her head emphatically. "What if I get a phone call from Belle Pink?" She said *Belle Pink* in a hushed, almost reverent whisper. "I wouldn't want to miss it . . . and I definitely don't want to be all sweaty and dirty when they call."

"Um, they aren't going to see what you look like if they call you," Midge said. "It's not like Skype."

Jughead pulled the brim of his baseball cap so it now faced backward. "Belle Pink? Is that a new girl at school?" he asked.

Nancy and Midge laughed as Veronica let out a long, slow sigh. "No, Jughead. Belle Pink isn't a *person*. Belle Pink is only the most *exclusive*, *fashionable*, and *chic* new store to open up at Riverdale Mall in, well, forever."

"She's right, man," Kevin said, nodding. "It's hot."

Veronica sat up straighter, brushing some imaginary sand off her arms. "I have literally been on pins and needles waiting to see if Belle Pink calls me."

At the mention of Belle Pink, Betty gave the ball an especially hard smack across the net. Belle Pink, Belle Pink, Belle Pink. Was that all her best friend could talk about? She knew Veronica was excited about the chance to work at the chic boutique, but Betty was getting a little tired of Veronica going on and on about how incredible a job at Belle Pink would look on her fashion school application.

Ever since Veronica decided she'd like to work at Belle Pink, it's become the only thing she can talk about, Betty thought, exasperated. *The girl has no clue how tough the job market is right now. And*

I should know! Betty frowned over at her best friend. If anyone needed a summer job, it wasn't Veronica.

Kevin stood up, took off his earbuds, and tossed his iPod on his towel. "Sorry," he said to Archie as they high-fived each other on the court. "I just needed a little power nap. Now I'm ready to kill."

"This is totally unfair," Midge complained, stomping her bare foot in the sand.

"Four against three is not cool with me," Nancy said, holding the ball against her hip.

"Hold on a minute." Betty walked across the court over to Veronica. "Come on, Ronnie. It's not going to kill you to put your phone down for a minute and play with us. Besides," she added, tilting her head toward the boys, "I know you don't want to give them something to gloat about for the rest of the summer. And with four against three now? There's definitely going to be some gloating."

Veronica hesitated, then grinned. "Okay, bestie. But just for one set." She put her phone on her towel and hopped to her feet.

"I mean, what are the chances they're going to call me the second I stop waiting for them to, right?" she asked as they walked toward the sand court.

They were halfway there when suddenly a blast of music came from behind them. "*She's a best dressed girlllll, she's got it in the bag.*"

"Ahhh!" Veronica shrieked. She turned and raced back to her beach towel, kicking up clouds of sand.

"Unbelievable," Betty muttered, shaking her head. She recognized the lyrics to "Best Dressed Girl," Belle Pink's signature song. Veronica had made it her ringtone yesterday when they'd arrived home after the mall.

Midge and Nancy ran over to join Veronica. They hovered anxiously as Veronica held the phone to her ear.

"Yes. Yes. Uh-huh. No. Yes. Really? Okay. Yes. Mm-hmm. Yes. Thank you!"

If the look on Veronica's face wasn't enough of an explanation, her instant jumping up and down said it all.

"Woo-hoo! Today, Belle Pink . . . tomorrow,

fashion designer to the stars!" Veronica said, her cheeks flushed pink with happiness.

Betty wanted to be happy for her friend. She really did. But it didn't seem fair that she had been trying to get a job for weeks, yet Veronica applied for one on a whim and actually got it. *No one ever said life was fair,* Betty thought, watching as Veronica hugged Midge and Nancy.

Betty thought back to her horoscope for the day. She was really into astrology—and at times like these, it sometimes helped her make sense of things. "There's nothing that you can't handle, Cancer," her daily horoscope had read. "So don't let the bumps in the road get you down. Steer around them and keep your head held high. Even the best of relationships can hit rocky patches."

I guess this is just a bump in the road, she decided. Time to be a true best friend and suck it up. She knew what she had to do. Slowly, she plodded through the hot sand toward Veronica.

"Congratulations. I'm really happy you got the job," Betty said, hugging her friend. "I know you're going to be an awesome salesperson."

"I'll totally give you my employee discount," Veronica promised, giving Betty a huge smile. Then a flicker of concern came over her face. "Oh, Betty. Don't worry. I know you're going to get a job this summer, too. It's all going to work out."

"Yeah, I just have to stay positive," Betty said, sounding more confident than she really felt inside. Her mom always said that if you act the way you want to feel, soon you'll start feeling the way you're acting.

"Yo, this is great and all, but we're kind of in the middle of a game," Reggie called impatiently. "Who's still in?"

"Just chill for a minute, Reggie. Jeez. Can't you see we're busy over here?" Nancy shouted back to him.

"Veronica's showing us this cute fashion app on her phone," Midge added as if that should have been obvious.

"Don't worry, Betty," Jughead said, coming over and slinging his arm around her slumped shoulders. "If nobody wants to hire you, you can hang out with us every day." He socked her in the arm. "That would be awesome!"

"Yeah. Awesome," Betty repeated, the words feeling thick in her throat. She rubbed her sore arm, looking from Jughead to Reggie to Archie to Kevin. Fist bumps. Shooting hoops. Playing video games in Reggie's basement. Working out. Endless jam sessions with The Archies in Archie's garage. Jokes about bodily functions. Was that really what this summer was going to be about?

I have got to find a summer job, Betty thought, more determined than ever. Because her horoscope was wrong. Hanging out with the guys all summer was definitely something she couldn't handle.

Chapter 3

"Bye! Have a good time!" Veronica called, waving to her parents as they walked hand in hand down their mansion's long stone sidewalk. The Lodges were on their way to a charity golf match at the Riverdale Country Club. She watched as their sleek black sedan pulled out onto the street, then she closed the heavy front door. Normally when her parents went out she did something fun, like have her friends over for a pool party or watch sappy romance movies with Betty. But not today. She was starting her first shift at Belle Pink in an hour.

Veronica jogged up the winding marble staircase and down the hallway to her room.

Clicking on some Lady Gaga, she went into her gigantic walk-in closet and began going through her clothes. The closet was larger than some of her friends' bedrooms. She had racks and drawers for clothes, shelves for her shoe collection, a full-length mirror—even a pink velvet couch and crystal chandelier.

A few minutes later she stood in front of the mirror and stared at her reflection. "Hmm. I'm not sure about this," she said to herself, turning from side to side. She was wearing a pair of black jeggings, a bright pink tank top, and gigantic silver hoop earrings. "I think maybe it's too casual."

She went over to a drawer, pulled out a gray vest, and slipped it on. Racks of jewelry sat on top of the dresser. "Maybe the silver one and purple one?" she said, slipping two necklaces over her head. Even though Veronica had already scored the job, it was vital that she made a good first impression.

She gave herself a critical once-over. "Argh. Now it looks like I'm trying too hard." She took off the necklaces and put on a newsboy cap she'd ordered online. Cute, but something still wasn't right. She started going through her closet again. "Maybe I should just pick something else out instead," she muttered.

Veronica was on her fourth outfit—a pair of adorable black denim jeans and a silky, sleeveless yellow top that looked great with her dark hair—when the intercom buzzer in her room went off. "Miss Veronica? Miss Betty is here to see you," said Melanie, one of the Lodges' maids.

"Thanks, Melanie," Veronica said. Maybe Betty could help her pick out something nice to wear.

"Hey," Betty said, walking into the closet. "Cool shirt." She sat down on Veronica's couch and leaned back on her hands.

"Hi, Betty. What's up? I could totally use your help right now . . . but you look a little depressed," Veronica said, peering at her friend. "Is everything okay?"

Betty blew out her breath. "I guess. I'm dropping off job applications at the pool, a garden supply store, and a vet's office. At this point I don't much care who hires me—I just want a job!" She squeezed her eyes shut. "I think I've applied at every single store in town."

Veronica felt a tiny bit guilty. Poor Betty had been applying for jobs with no luck. *And I got the first and only job I applied for,* Veronica thought. That definitely had to be upsetting to Betty. Then Veronica got a terrific idea. "You know, Betty, my dad has some serious connections in this town," she told her friend.

Betty opened her eyes, looking confused. "Uh-huh," she said, not sure where the conversation was going.

"Well . . . all he would have to do is make a few phone calls and bingo!" Veronica snapped her fingers in Betty's face. "You could get a job just like that." Why hadn't she thought of this sooner? Betty needed a job, and Mr. Lodge could get her one. Easy-peasy.

But Betty didn't seem to see things in quite the same way.

"Thanks a lot, Veronica, but I think I can

get a job on my own," Betty said, looking at her in disbelief. "I don't need your dad to step in and get me one."

"Um, no offense, but I think you kind of do," Veronica said. "Not to be mean or anything, but you haven't exactly had a lot of offers, Betty. You've said so yourself."

A flash of anger lit up Betty's face. "I can't believe you would say that to me. I am a really hard worker. And with my grades, I should be more than able to get a job on my own," she said, her voice rising. "A real job—one where I have to use my brain. Not some—some fluffy fashion job."

Fluffy fashion job? That sounded suspiciously like an insult to Veronica. "Well," she said haughtily, "my job at Belle Pink might seem small—but small steps are what take you to big places. Everyone has to start somewhere."

Holding her head high, she walked past Betty to the mirror. Quickly she pulled her hair up into a high ponytail and snapped on an elastic. Then she walked over to her shoe shelves and grabbed a pair of uncomfortable yet supertrendy metallic sandals.

"I don't know if you want to stay here and hang out by yourself, but I've got to go," she said, feeling annoyed, angry, and kind of badly for her friend all at the same time. She threw her phone, hairbrush, gum, and wallet into a large gray leather satchel and slung it over her shoulder. "Because unlike you, *I've* got to get to work."

XOXO

After Veronica left, Betty sat there stewing in her best friend's big closet, wondering what had just happened. How did a simple visit to Veronica's house turn into a fight? Betty knew deep down that Veronica was just trying to help her. She knew she wasn't trying to hurt her feelings—but still, it was kind of insulting. Did she really think Betty couldn't get a job on her own?

Maybe she couldn't. Maybe she would spend all summer filling out job applications, going from store to store, and listening to

Veronica map out her career as a fashion designer.

"Miss Betty?" Melanie knocked lightly on the closet door. "Are you all right? Would you like a glass of lemonade?"

"Oh! No. Thanks. I was just, um, leaving." Betty managed to give Melanie a smile before walking out of Veronica's room. Just then her phone buzzed in her pocket. It was a text from Archie.

Hey . . . want to meet me at Pop's? I'm starving.

Betty smiled. Maybe lunch with Archie Andrews was just what she needed.

Sounds great. See you there. 20 minutes?

XOXO

Pop's Chocklit Shoppe was one of the most popular hangouts in Riverdale. Everyone went there. And today it looked like literally everyone in town *was* there. When Betty walked inside the restaurant, she couldn't believe how crowded it was. The soda fountain counter stools were all taken, every booth was filled, and there were at least twenty people waiting for a table.

"Yo, Betty! Over here!" Archie waved from a spot near the wall. She waved and made her way through the crowd.

"Hi, Archie," she said, lighting up when she saw him. He had on a pair of long black basketball shorts and a sleeveless red shirt that said PLAY HARD OR GO HOME. "So what's going on? Since when is Pop's this crowded on a Thursday afternoon?"

Archie shrugged. "Dunno. It's been like this ever since I walked in. Hey, Pop!" he called as the owner of the restaurant walked past. "This is crazy, huh?"

Pop Tate looked completely frazzled. His apron was covered in chocolate, and his forehead was glistening with sweat. "The air conditioner over at Sam's Subs stopped working—and they won't get it up and running for weeks. The part they need to fix it is on back order." Pop ran his hand nervously through his hair. "So not only do I have all my regular customers like you, I've got Sam's customers as well."

"That's good for business, then," Betty said. She knew Sam's was a big rival of Pop's.

But Pop didn't hear her. He had already hurried off to the kitchen.

"So how's the job hunt going?" Archie asked.

Betty grimaced. "Don't ask."

Archie laughed and squeezed Betty's shoulder. "Don't worry, Coop. It's going to work out. Veronica found a job, and—"

"Please don't remind me. And can we not talk about her? We're kind of in a fight at the moment."

Archie shook his head. "Girl drama. Some things never change."

Betty rolled her eyes. Archie had had to suffer through a lot of Betty's ups and downs with Veronica over the years. She knew that eventually they would make up. But for now she was annoyed with her . . . and was going to stay that way for the whole day. Maybe even the rest of the week.

Finally they got a booth and Betty flipped open a menu. Even though she had been there a million times, she still liked to look at the menu.

"What are you in the mood for?" Archie asked.

Betty shrugged, resting her elbows on the Formica tabletop. "I'm thinking a turkey burger and onion rings with a chocolate milkshake. With extra whipped cream."

"Excellent choice," Archie said with a nod.

Georgette, Betty's favorite waitress, came over to take their order. "Sorry to keep you waiting, guys," she apologized. Her blond bun was coming undone. Wayward tendrils framed her face. "I'm just getting slammed today. Way too many tables to handle!"

"Yeah, it's wild in here. Why doesn't Pop hire more waitresses?" Archie asked after ordering a cheeseburger and fries.

Georgette sighed. "I ask myself that every day. But then I know the answer. This place is Pop's baby, kids. Pop is really picky about who works at the Chocklit Shoppe. He only employs people he's known a long time. People he can trust like family."

Then she hurried off to place their order.

"It's totally obvious, Betty. Why don't you apply for a job here?"

Betty blinked at him. "Doing what?"

Archie snorted. "Betty. Take a look around the place. What do you think? A waitress job!"

"But I have never been a waitress before," Betty blurted out. She'd never even considered waitressing as an option.

"You heard what Georgette said," Archie went on, growing more and more animated. "Pop knows you, and you need a job."

Betty thought for a moment. "I don't know, Archie," she said slowly. "I'm not really sure I could be a waitress."

"Sure you could, hon," came a voice from behind them. It was Georgette. She slid a plate of delicious-smelling food in front of each of them. "Let me talk to Pop."

"Um, okay," Betty said, sliding the wrapper

off her straw. Suddenly her stomach was filled with butterflies. She'd wanted a summer job . . . but could she handle being a waitress?

"It's in the bag, Coop," Archie said, picking up his burger. "It's gonna be a sweet gig. Me and Jughead will be your best customers."

And by the time she and Archie were finishing their lunches, it was all set.

Pop had hired Betty on the spot. She was going to be a waitress at Pop's Chocklit Shoppe.

And she was going to start tomorrow.

Chapter 4

Veronica pulled her phone out of her purse and checked the time. Ten forty-five. Perfect. *Better to be fifteen minutes early than one minute late,* she thought, her pulse quickening as she approached the pink-awninged storefront of Belle Pink.

"If there's a better way to spend my summer vacation, I don't know what it is," Veronica said to herself as she took one metallic-sandal step into the store. She thought back to her conversation with Betty. All she had been trying to do was help her best friend, and instead they ended up in a fight.

She shook off the memory. Betty would come around, right? She'd deal with that later.

For now, she had her *job* to think about.

Loud, cool French rock music was blasting from the cute little Eiffel Tower–shaped speakers. Veronica closed her eyes and inhaled the sweet, intoxicating smell of Belle Pink's signature scent, Femme Fatale. Then she opened her eyes and walked through the aisles. She laid her hand on a faux fur vest, then reached out to touch a leopard jersey tank top. Veronica gazed around the trendy boutique in wonder. "This is going to be the best summer of my life!" she squealed, not caring if anyone heard her.

Veronica walked to the back cash registers. She recognized the woman standing there—thin, with short dark hair, black-framed glasses, and bright red lipstick. She was Jane, the store's manager.

"*Bonjour,* Veronica," Jane said, giving Veronica a big smile. "We're so glad to have you on board. Come with me into the back."

Veronica's heart raced a little faster. She'd been in the store only five minutes and already she was being taken to the inner sanctum! But when they walked into the backroom, it wasn't as glamorous as Veronica thought it was going to be. There was a chart on the wall with what Veronica guessed were employee names and what hours they were working that week. An old, rickety-looking wooden table was littered with magazines, crumpled newspapers, and some leftover Chinese food containers. There was a mini-refrigerator covered with poetry magnets. Some dirty coffee cups. A coat rack with sweaters and jackets. And lots and lots of boxes.

Jane showed Veronica where she would need to sign in for her shift and where her hours would be posted. "The restroom is over there," Jane said, pointing to a dingy-looking door that said SALLE DE BAIN. "It's for employees only." She went through a bunch of rules and things to remember. Then she handed Veronica a cute metallic, pink name tag.

"I love it," Veronica said, clipping it to her yellow top. "Oops, I mean, *j'adore*."

Veronica followed Jane back out onto the "selling floor" as Jane called it. The doors had just opened. Veronica's heart raced a little faster. That meant customers would soon be pouring in. And it would be up to Veronica to help them find the perfect little black dress . . . the right pair of skinny pants . . . the trendiest sweater . . . Riverdale's female population would be counting on her.

Veronica sighed with happiness.

"Veronica, I'd like you to meet Lola," Jane said. "Lola has worked at Belle Pink for six months. She's going to show you the ropes."

Veronica smiled at Lola. She was a little shorter than Veronica, with shoulder-length straight brown hair and pretty hazel eyes. She had on a pair of blue capris, blue ballet flats, and a kind-of-blah white top. Veronica thought it was kind of boring and unimpressive for someone on the staff of Belle Pink. *I guess she's just a good salesperson.* Veronica glanced down at her own outfit. She had added a striped, puff-sleeve plaid gray jacket over her yellow silk top and black denim jeans along with a grosgrain and chain necklace her mother had found in Paris.

"At Belle Pink it's important that all the clothing tables are perfectly organized. And that means everything is perfectly folded," Lola said. She held up a pair of jeans. "The seam and hemlines need to match, and the zipper should be up and the button buttoned." Veronica watched as Lola expertly folded a pair of jeans on the table, pressing out any possible creases. "Like that."

"Um . . . when are we going to start helping customers?" Veronica asked Lola after she demonstrated on four more pairs of pants and had Veronica do it as well.

"First things first," Lola said a little primly. They moved on to shirts. Lola showed Veronica how to fold sweaters. Long-sleeved tops. T-shirts. Tank tops. And she began every lesson the same way. "At Belle Pink it's important . . ." By the sixth demonstration, Veronica could feel her eyes beginning to glaze over.

Then Veronica noticed a grandmother-type woman in a frumpy green sweater walk in the store looking a little lost.

"*Bonjour!* Welcome to Belle Pink," Lola said automatically. "Please let me know if I can help you find something *magnifique.*"

"I'm just browsing today. Thank you," the woman said, going over to the sweaters they had just folded. She picked the top one up, looked at it . . . and dropped it back onto the pile. Then she went through the stack of T-shirts and did the same thing.

Veronica frowned. She was about to storm over and give that woman a piece of her mind when Lola stopped her.

"You can't let that bother you," Lola told Veronica. "It happens all the time. Every day. Every hour. It's as if people wait for you to fold things just so they can demolish them."

"That's so frustrating!" Veronica said.

"At Belle Pink it's important not to get frustrated," Lola said, squaring her shoulders.

Apparently there were lots of things that were important at Belle Pink. And Lola knew each and every one of them.

The store was starting to get busier, so Veronica was surprised when Lola asked her to follow her to the back room.

"We've got a lot of boxes to get through," Lola said, pointing to the towering stack of boxes Veronica had seen earlier. "The box cutters are kept on the desk. You need to open each box along the side first and then slit the top—that way you won't slice through any merchandise inside and accidentally damage something. Once you get everything opened and remove the clothes, you take each item to the steamer and get it ready to put on the floor. At Belle Pink, it's important that all our clothes are freshly pressed . . ."

Veronica stood in shocked silence as Lola outlined the entire process. "But . . . aren't there stock people to do that kind of thing?" Veronica protested when she was finished. She wasn't trying to complain or anything, but Veronica didn't think opening boxes was really the best use of her talents.

Lola smiled at Veronica. "Yes, there are stock people to do that." She pointed up at the schedule. And there, under the category *Stock and Steam,* was one name: VERONICA.

XOXO

It had been the slowest six hours of Veronica's life. Fold. Stack. Watch as a customer picks up the just-folded items and unfolds them. Seethe inside but smile at customer. Walk over. Refold. Restack. Over. And over. And over. And those twenty minutes were the high point of her shift. The rest of it had been spent in the back room slicing open large cardboard boxes.

Veronica got tiny bits of cardboard all over her black jeans. She'd dropped a box on her foot. The steamer had made her hot and sweaty. And she'd chipped her new manicure trying to pull open one of the boxes.

All in the name of fashion, I guess, she thought, walking dejectedly out of the store after signing out. Jane had left, Lola was working the cash register, and two other employees had shown up for their shifts.

"Hey, Veronica!"

She turned at the sound of a familiar voice. It was Kevin.

"How was it?" he asked, jogging over to her. His hair was wet—probably from the beach—and he had on long, blue board shorts and a gray T-shirt. "Make lots of big commissions today, huh?"

Veronica shook her head. "Commission? Uh, I was barely even allowed out of the back room. They kept me there the whole time like . . . like a prisoner." She told Kevin about rule-abiding Lola. "I spent the entire day opening boxes and steaming clothes. Anytime a customer came in, Lola ran right over and began reciting the rulebook."

Kevin laughed. "All in a day's work, Veronica. Now you get to see how the other half lives."

Veronica didn't appreciate that comment. Just because her father was rich didn't mean she was clueless about working for a living. She was about to tell Kevin that when he held up his hands in mock protest.

"Hey now. Don't get upset. I'm just

kidding around. I'm sure it's going to get better. I mean, it can't get worse, right?"

Veronica shrugged. "I guess not." She looked down at her tired, aching feet. "And it was a total waste of cute shoes, too."

"So if you were a prisoner back there, I guess it's safe to say you didn't see him," Kevin said, wriggling his eyebrows. Veronica looked in the direction Kevin indicated with his chin. And there, in the computer store across from Belle Pink in the mall, was one of the hottest guys Veronica had ever seen. He was organizing a spinner rack in the front of the store. His chiseled arms reached to hang up cell phone skins. A girl with short, tousled black hair in a raven-colored tank dress was standing outside the store watching—or rather ogling—him. It was Midge Klump.

Veronica sucked in her breath. Her stomach filled with butterflies.

Maybe today wasn't going to be a waste of cute shoes after all.

Chapter 5

"I saw him first," Midge said with a huff.

"Technically, Kevin saw him first. But Kevin had to run, so now he's entirely up for grabs," Veronica told her, crossing her arms. "And, technically, you have a boyfriend. One Moose Mason, to be exact."

Veronica had walked over and joined a surprised Midge. The two girls were now standing outside the store's big, glass windows, pretending to be interested in the window display.

"Just because I have a boyfriend doesn't mean I'm not allowed to look," Midge retorted. "It doesn't hurt to flirt."

"Okay," Veronica said, lowering her

voice. "I've got an idea." She leaned over and whispered into Midge's ear.

Midge grinned. "You're on, Veronica. Just don't take it too hard when you lose."

Veronica surreptitiously pulled out her compact and slicked on some raspberry-colored lip gloss. Then she finger-fluffed her beautiful long, dark hair and brushed the lint off her jeans as best she could.

"Trying hard? *So* not cool," Midge said, shaking her head so that her chandelier earrings jingled.

Veronica ignored her. "Watch and learn, Midge," she whispered, sauntering inside the store as Midge tagged alongside her. "Watch and learn." Veronica couldn't help it: Guys just fell at her feet.

"Hi there," a perky female employee said to the two girls. "Can I help you? We're running some great promotions today!"

"Hmmm. Not yet," Midge said as Veronica breezed past her. "Thanks, though." They walked a little farther into the store.

Veronica clutched Midge's arm. "There

he is," she hissed, spotting the hot guy. He was showing a customer a touch-screen phone. "Remember what I said. It's important that we act natural." She leaned against a beam, jutted out her hip, and gave Midge her biggest, most high-wattage smile.

"Yeah, that's real natural, Veronica," Midge said through gritted teeth. "Almost as natural as your hair color."

Veronica's eyes blazed. "I can't believe you would even—"

"Hi, ladies. Need any help?"

Veronica sucked in her breath. It was Hot Guy. And he was even hotter up close. He had shaggy brown hair, warm brown eyes, and a cute, slightly crooked smile that made him look instantly approachable. And even though he was wearing a store employee outfit of khakis and a green T-shirt, he wore the latest sneakers and a cool hemp bracelet. Veronica was sure that when he was able to pick out his own clothes, he had excellent fashion taste.

"Hey, what's going on? Um, I'm interested

in a new laptop," Midge said, smiling nervously at him. She tucked a stray piece of hair behind her ear. "What can you tell me about this one?" She hesitated and then pointed to a random laptop.

Veronica watched intently as the guy—whose name tag said LIAM—explained the features of the various laptops. In between all the information about processors and graphics and pixels and battery life, she waited to see if there were any sparks between him and Midge. Although Liam was superfriendly and knowledgeable, she didn't detect a single spark of romantic interest in poor Midge on his behalf.

"So you think this one would be a good choice?" Veronica asked, pointing to a thin silver model. She tossed her hair back flirtatiously.

Liam nodded. "Definitely. Not only is it light, it's beautifully streamlined."

Veronica beamed, batting her eyelashes. "Oh, wow."

Midge jabbed her finger into Veronica's

ribs as Liam walked them over to another display. "He's talking about the computer, Veronica. Not you."

"Now this one is a beauty," he said, holding up another laptop. Veronica felt her breath catch in her throat. When he said *beauty*, there was no doubt he was looking straight at her.

"I wasn't really in the market for a new laptop, but after seeing all these new models, maybe I should be," Veronica said, moving closer to Liam. She pointed to the laptop. "Can you show me how it works?"

"Veronica, I thought you hated using a laptop." Midge cut in suddenly—and very rudely, Veronica thought—as she glared at her. "Isn't that what you were telling Archie and Reggie last week?"

Veronica gave Midge a withering look. "That's right, Midgie. I told my *friends* that I hated the laptop I had." She turned back to Liam. "If I had one like this, though, I wouldn't be able to put it down!"

Liam nodded. "Yeah, absolutely. This is

the best laptop on the market. It's got up to nine hours of battery life, superfast graphics, and it's energy efficient."

"Say no more," Veronica said. *Because I just want to gaze at your adorable face.* But of course she didn't say that. "Wrap it up, please. I'll take it."

Liam looked surprised. "Uh, are you sure? Don't you want to know how much it costs first?"

Veronica beamed at him. "I'm sure it's fine. Let's just go ring it up."

"That was beneath even you, Veronica," Midge hissed in her ear as they followed Liam toward the cash register. "Buying your way to a guy's heart? Real classy."

"Oh please," Veronica said, brushing her off. Normally she really liked Midge— unless she was being annoying. Like she was right now. "Whether you believe me or not, I really do need a new laptop. You're just jealous that he's obviously into me and not you."

Midge shrugged. "He works here. You're

a customer with money. Of course he's going to act like he likes you. But don't think you have it in the bag just yet."

"Shhh," Veronica whispered as they arrived at the counter. She took out her American Express Black card and handed it over. For a moment she thought about Betty and how important getting a laptop was to her friend. She knew it wasn't really fair that she could just come in and buy one while her best friend had to scrimp and save all summer long.

But if she'd let me, I'd buy her one in a second, Veronica thought guiltily. She loved being generous with her friends, but she'd learned over the years that her true friends really didn't feel comfortable with her buying them gifts or things they needed. So she had stopped offering, even if it would make everyone's lives easier.

"I've never seen a card like this," Liam said, examining Veronica's credit card. "It's really cool."

"My father gave it to me," Veronica

explained. "He was one of the first people in the world to get one. You have to spend a certain amount on it or something. I forget."

Liam rang up the purchase as another employee put Veronica's new laptop in a shopping bag and handed it to her.

"I hope you love it," Liam told her, nodding toward the bag. "If you have any questions on how to use some of the functions . . . or, uh, anything, you can just give me a call." He grinned sheepishly. "I put my store contact card in the bag."

"Oh great!" Veronica said happily, resisting the urge to smirk in Midge's face. *Looks like I* literally *have it in the bag after all.* "I just started working at Belle Pink . . . the store across from you. So maybe we'll see each other sometime."

"That would be cool," Liam said. He gave a little wave. "Bye."

"Bye," Veronica said, giving him one last smile as Midge barely lifted her chin in a halfhearted nod.

"Sorry it didn't go your way, Midge," Veronica said, feeling as light and bubbly as a glass of seltzer. "But you and Moose make such a cute couple," she reminded her friend. "Harmless flirting is fine, but I just can't see you going out with anyone but him. I'm sorry, but it's true."

Midge gave Veronica a stony glare . . . and then she laughed. "As much as I hate to say it, you're probably right."

The drudgery of the day had washed away, and now all Veronica could think about was working her next shift. *Maybe Liam will be working then, too!*

"Easy come, easy go," Midge said with an exaggerated sigh. "I just wish I could warn the poor guy . . . from what I've heard, dating Veronica Lodge should come with an instruction manual."

Spoiled, selfish, bratty . . . Veronica had heard all the mean labels before. But they didn't bother her. Not one bit.

"Why should I apologize for being a confident person? I'm just a girl who knows

what she wants," she said simply, swinging the
shopping bag back and forth in her hand.

And right now she wanted Liam.

Chapter 6

"Here you go: one chef's salad, one order of french fries, and a cheeseburger." Betty smiled brightly at her customers: a middle-aged couple wearing matching blue T-shirts.

The woman frowned. "I told you I wanted the blue cheese dressing on the side."

The man shook his head. "And I ordered a grilled cheese."

"Oh, I'm sorry," Betty apologized, picking up his platter. "You're right."

"Of course I am," the man said, chuckling. He shot a self-righteous look at his wife. "I am the customer."

What a dork. But still, Betty managed a smile and then turned and dashed off.

Today was her second day on the job, and Betty couldn't believe how hard being a waitress was—much harder than Betty had ever thought, and Betty had thought it was going to be hard. Being a customer at Pop's Chocklit Shoppe was a completely different experience from being an employee.

And right now I wish I was a customer, Betty thought enviously as some girls she recognized from school came in laughing and joking around. They sat in Georgette's section.

Betty sighed. But if she wanted a new laptop, she was going to have to give up being a customer for a while.

Betty had spent most of yesterday training under Pop's watchful eye. He told her that normally he would never put someone brand-new on as a waitress—he'd have the newbie shadow a more experienced staffer for at least a week. But because Pop's was so busy right now, there wasn't time to do things the normal way. Betty was just going to have to learn as she went.

And she had a lot of learning to do.

"Miss? Utensils?" a woman prompted, gesturing to the table.

"Oh, sure. Sorry!" Betty hurried into the kitchen.

"Betty, the food isn't supposed to come back once it leaves my kitchen," barked Mikey, the cook.

Betty swallowed, trying not to sound nervous. "I, uh, made a mistake. I ordered a cheeseburger instead of a grilled cheese for one of my tables."

Frowning and muttering some not so very nice words, Mikey took back the unwanted cheeseburger and made Betty a grilled cheese.

"They did want American cheese, right?" he asked, handing the sandwich over.

"Oh . . . yes. Mm-hmm. American," Betty said, even though she had no idea. For all she knew, they wanted Vermont cheddar. *Note to self: Ask customers what kind of cheese they want when they order cheese.*

The right sandwich now in hand, Betty ran back out to deliver it. On her way, she dropped off a place setting to the woman who needed one.

People were so aggravating. Drink refills, extra ketchup, more napkins . . . couldn't anyone just be content with what they had? No one seemed satisfied. And why couldn't people order what they wanted at once instead of adding things once the order was complete?

Betty had to carry a tray full of chocolate milkshakes out to a table of rowdy nine-year-old boys celebrating a soccer victory. For once in her life, being smart didn't matter—carrying a tray heavier than ten backpacks without spilling its contents was what counted.

"All right!" the boys cheered as Betty carefully lowered the tray and began doling out the shakes.

As Betty handed over the last one, she wiped her hands on her soiled apron and smiled. She hadn't spilled a single one.

It almost made up for the tray of sodas she had dropped that morning.

On her way into the kitchen, Georgette signaled to her. "You've got some important customers at table twenty-three," she said, raising an eyebrow. "They requested to sit in your section."

Who could that be? Betty warily turned to look. And there at table twenty-three were Jughead and Archie. They gave her a wave. Betty was happy and nervous all at once.

On the one hand, it was nice to have two guys she was so close with show up while she was working. Betty knew they would be nothing but nice to her. On the other hand, she didn't want to make a fool of herself in front of them. The soda-tray-dropping incident from before had been completely humiliating. Pop had just laughed it off, but Betty hadn't been laughing.

She had felt like sobbing instead.

XOXO

"So," Jughead asked, leaning back in the booth and stretching his legs out, "what do you recommend here? Any specials today?"

Betty gave him an exasperated stare.

"You have got to be kidding me," she said in a low, measured voice. She'd rushed over to take her friends' orders, assuming they'd make it nice and easy for her. She should have known that wasn't in Jughead's DNA. "Just order something, Jughead! Can't you see how crazy it is in here?"

Archie was laughing behind his menu. "Just get me a chocolate shake and some cheese fries, please," he told her.

But Jughead wasn't giving up. "Are there any specials today?" he persisted, crossing his arms. His beanie slipped down his forehead. "I'm a growing boy, Betty. I'm pretty hungry."

Archie snorted. "Man, when aren't you hungry?" Jughead's never-ending appetite and amazing metabolism were well-known around school. No matter how much food Jughead ate, he never gained an ounce of weight. Jughead was still the same lanky, skinny guy that he always was.

"Okay," Betty said, whipping out her order pad. She began scribbling as she spoke. "One cup of homemade chicken noodle soup, one medium-well cheeseburger on an onion bun, french fries, and a soda. Sound good?"

Jughead thought for a moment, then patted his flat stomach. "Add a slice of warm apple pie, my friend, and we're good to go."

"You did bring your wallet, right, Jughead?" Betty asked, cocking an eyebrow. She had known Jughead for a long time, and not only did he have a huge appetite, he sometimes ordered more food than he could pay for. She wouldn't put it past him to stiff her on the check.

Now Jughead looked insulted. "If this is how you treat your customers, I might have to find another place to eat."

She did not have time for Jughead's nonsense today. Blowing out her breath, Betty tucked her pen behind her ear and hurried to put the order in and then go to her next table.

She'd just have to worry about Jughead's

finances or lack thereof later. *Besides, if he can't pay his bill, I can use my tip money and he can pay me back.* "Miss? Can you take our order?" a customer called impatiently. Betty sighed and trotted over to the table. *That is, if I get any tips.*

XOXO

"This is it, Jughead. And I mean it," Betty said, banging the bottle of ketchup down on the table. She had a lot of tables to take care of—but all she was doing was running back and forth for one of them: Jughead and Archie's.

"Jeez, testy much?" Jughead said, shaking his head as he unscrewed the bottle and poured a gigantic puddle of ketchup on his plate. "All I asked for was a bottle of ketchup," he said sadly. "What a crazy request."

"Maybe if you didn't use half a bottle it would last longer," Betty said.

She was definitely at her wit's end. Soda refills. Extra coleslaw. Extra ketchup. Extra mayo. Food that was too cold. Could she bring another straw? And that was just for Jughead!

"Sorry," Archie mouthed as Jughead dug into his fries. "You know Jughead. I promise—we'll leave a big tip." Then he reached for Betty's hand. "I was hoping we'd get to spend some time together this summer."

"That would be nice," Betty said, though she wasn't sure she was up to being "on" again with Archie. They'd kind of taken a break for the past few months or so. Dating Archie caused a lot of drama with Veronica—drama she wasn't in the mood for. "I'm working a lot of hours, though."

"Text me," Archie told her, raising his eyebrows.

"Okay," Betty relented. Veronica had texted her earlier—something about a cute guy she'd met at the mall. So maybe Veronica wouldn't mind if Betty started hanging out with Archie this summer. She'd just take things slowly.

"Hey, Betty?" Jughead was calling her.

"Do you think you could bring me some of that chipotle mayo? That tastes incredible on the fries."

"I have two words for you," she said tartly.

"Sure thing?" Jughead guessed hopefully.

Betty smiled very hard. "Big. Tip." Then she stormed off.

Chapter 7

Veronica pulled her pristine white convertible with the tan leather seats into a shaded parking spot at the mall. Then she pulled out her phone from her bag and punched in Betty's number. The two best friends hadn't stayed angry with each other for too long. Life was too short.

And so was Veronica's patience with the way things were going at Belle Pink. She had worked every day for the past week—and she had spent each and every one of those days in the stock room. She had the split nails to prove it.

"Hey, you," she said when Betty answered the phone. "What's going on?"

"I just woke up," Betty mumbled sleepily. "I was having a bad dream about spilling drinks on people." Then she groaned. "Wait a minute. That wasn't a dream. It really happened."

"I know it's tough," Veronica said. "But just think! By the time school rolls around, you'll be rockin' a supercool laptop."

"If I live that long," Betty moaned.

Veronica laughed as she got out of her car and walked through the crowded parking lot. She passed by the department store, turned left at the fro-yo shop, and passed the cluster of tables at the food court. Coming to the mall to work every day had quickly started to feel like her everyday routine. But that was why she absolutely had to change the way she spent her day. "Gotta go, cupcake. Text me later, 'kay?" She clicked off her phone and tossed it in her canvas bag.

"I've got to prove to Jane what an asset having me on staff really is," Veronica said to herself. She had taken great pains to look trendy and cool every day. Today she had on a sleeveless black silky top, except she—trendsetter that she was—was wearing it as a dress, along with textured stockings and high-heeled ankle booties. She had to admit—she looked exquisite.

Filled with determination, she strode in the entrance. *"Bonjour!"* she said to one customer. "Ahh, *très jolie,*" she said to two middle school–aged girls who were trying on some scarves. Jane gave her a wave from the cash register.

"Hello, everyone," she said cheerfully, walking into the backroom. "Everyone" consisted of one other person: Lola. As usual, she looked totally humdrum: gray T-shirt, black skirt, black ballet flats, tiny stud earrings, and no makeup.

"So today Jane thought you should spend the day with me on the sales floor," Lola told her, blinking.

"Really? That's so awesome!" Veronica squealed. She put on her name tag. "Let's get out onto the floor and make some fashion happen!"

The two girls walked toward the front of the store. "You get to fold clothes today while I help customers," Lola explained.

Veronica skidded to a stop. "I 'get' to fold clothes?" She frowned. "I don't really think that's fair. Can't we both help customers?" Veronica knew that if she was only given a chance, she could sell a ton of clothes at Belle Pink—and make Riverdale an even more fashionable place to live.

Lola shook her head. "At Belle Pink it's important that employees work at every job so that they have an understanding and appreciation of all the responsibilities here."

"*Oui, oui,*" Veronica snapped, walking over to a table of T-shirts. It looked like a small tsunami had blown through. Automatically Veronica started folding. *This is kind of scary,* she thought. *I can actually do this without even thinking about it now. I've practically turned into a robot!*

Then she had an idea. Just because she was folding clothes didn't mean she couldn't still help customers. She would just have to be a little more outgoing and creative about it, that was all.

"Those scarves are cute on you, but you know what would be cuter?" Veronica called over. "Those hats that are on the rack over by the wall."

"Do you think so?" one of the girls asked. "We weren't sure."

"Oh, definitely." Veronica nodded. "They can totally take an okay outfit to amazing."

The girls hurried over to the hats as Veronica smiled to herself.

"Excuse me, do you have this in my size?" a woman asked, holding up a tiny empire-waist blouse.

Veronica shook her head. "That blouse doesn't come in your size," she said.

"It doesn't?" The woman looked confused.

Veronica gave the woman a warm, friendly smile. "That top is better for teenagers. A woman of your age needs something a little more . . . sophisticated."

"Um, Veronica?" Lola had materialized at her side. "Can I talk to you for a minute?"

"I wish I could, but I'm kind of busy," Veronica said sweetly. "Now how about this?" she asked, turning back to the customer. She held up a more age-appropriate top. "This is guaranteed to make you look like a million bucks."

"Well . . . I guess I'll try it," the woman said, taking the shirt from Veronica. "But I still liked the first one."

Veronica shrugged. "It's up to you, of course. But I think you'll thank me later."

"Veronica!" Lola hissed as the woman continued to browse. "You can't talk to customers like that. At Belle Pink—"

"We want to help every customer look her best, right?" Veronica stared fixedly at her. "So that's what I'm trying to do while I fold all these beautiful T-shirts." She gave Lola a bright smile and kept on folding.

When her lunch break came, Veronica could hardly believe it. Her shift had flown by! It was definitely a lot more rewarding to help customers find the right clothes than it was opening boxes. Of course, she *had* hurt a few people's feelings. She didn't mean to, but it wouldn't really be all that helpful of her to let customers try on and maybe even purchase things that were unflattering.

"I mean, I'm just saying that skinny jeans are not your friend," she had told one girl, sending her scurrying for the dressing room with a pair of flattering flares. "Would you really want to let people see you in a blouse that's that low-cut?" she had asked a woman who was old enough to be her mother. "I think not."

"Honesty is the best policy," she had huffed to Lola each time she'd tried to stop her.

"Not if it's losing us customers," Lola had retorted as two girls walked quickly out of the shop after Veronica told them their hips were too wide for the dresses they were looking at.

Veronica simply shrugged. "I won't be responsible for fashion disasters on the streets of Riverdale," she whispered as Lola walked away. "I'd rather wear last season's styles than do that!"

"Today you're going to do something a little different," Lola told Veronica. It was the next day, and Veronica and Lola were back on the selling floor. "Today, you're going to change the mannequins in the front of the store."

Veronica's eyes lit up. That sounded right up her alley—much better than opening boxes and steaming clothes. Being original, taking fashion risks—that was what she excelled at.

"That sounds so cool," she told Lola. "I love expressing myself creatively." Her mind was a blur of design ideas. "We could use those cute skirts that came in yesterday with tank tops . . . or do a total season mismatch—like sweaters with shorts and fur coats with flip-flops. That would totally catch people's eyes!"

Lola had been holding a clipboard with papers attached. She held it out. "That sounds interesting, but you won't be doing that. At Belle Pink it's important to follow the planogram. That way all Belle Pink stores are the same, no matter if you're in Riverdale or New York City."

"The planogram?" Veronica repeated. "What's that?"

"It's your new bible." Lola shoved it into Veronica's hands. "This diagram details what clothes are to go on the mannequins—nothing is left to chance. Every Belle Pink store has the same number of mannequins at the front, and they are all wearing the same things. Right down to the jewelry," Lola finished, a satisfied smile on her face.

Veronica was anything but. She frowned. "I have to follow a plan to dress a mannequin? Where's the fun in that?"

She thought back to when she was a little girl, playing dress-up with Betty and their dolls. They'd put on berets and capes and borrow her mother's high heels . . . they'd looked ridiculous, but it had kept them entertained for hours. Even the memory still made her smile.

"There are just way too many rules here," Veronica said, staring at the planogram. She could feel her shoulders slump. "You're taking the fun right out of fashion."

"I'm sorry," Veronica said as she buttoned up a pink shirt on the mannequin. "I know you'd much rather be wearing a sequined little tank top and a cute miniskirt, but that's not on the planogram, so we can't do it!" She patted the mannequin's stiff, white arm. "Don't worry, though. You only have to wear this for one week." Veronica had been surprised to see that not only were there specific things the mannequins had to wear, but there were even dates that spelled out how long they had to wear things and when they got to change.

"And that's someone's job," she muttered, shaking her head. She stole a glance back into the store. Lola was helping a girl find a pair of jeans.

I just know she's jealous of me, Veronica thought, moving over to the next mannequin. *She's definitely threatened by someone with such originality.*

Suddenly her eyes widened. There, across the way in the computer store, was Liam! She had seen him only once since that day with Kevin—and he'd been so busy helping a customer that she'd given up trying to catch his attention.

Today, though, he was looking right at Veronica.

She waved and he waved back. "Ooh, you are such a cutie pie!" Veronica said. He had on the store outfit—the khakis and the green T-shirt—but the way he tucked his hair behind his ears combined with his uneven smile—it was just so adorable.

Veronica loved having an audience. She began dressing mannequin number two, slipping a blue bandage dress over her head. "Girl, you are going to drive the boys crazy with this one," she said as if she were having a real conversation. When she looked over at Liam, he was laughing.

Veronica laughed, too. Flirting was so much fun!

She studied the planogram. "Now, it says

here that you're supposed to wear sunglasses and a scarf. But there's no reason the scarf can't be wrapped around your head turban style, now is there?" She styled the mannequin as outrageously as she could, moving the mannequin's arms so it looked like it was waving at Liam. Then she snuck a peek at Liam. Sure enough, he was watching her.

He shook his head. "You're crazy!" he mouthed, grinning.

Veronica gave him a happy shrug. Mannequin number three was wearing jeans and a T-shirt. "There isn't a funky hat or platform sandals in the planogram for you . . . but who says we can't add them?" she asked, covering the mannequin's jet-black hair with a red fedora.

"I'm not sure what's going on up here, but remember, Veronica, you have to follow the planogram," Lola said, marching over to her. Her face looked pinched and annoyed as she reached out and yanked the fedora off the mannequin's head.

Veronica groaned inwardly. It was like

Lola had a sixth sense for when someone else was having a good moment. *Oh my goodness! It looks like Veronica Lodge is having fun at her job! I must put a stop to it!* She looked over at the computer store, but Liam had disappeared.

Lola waved the planogram under her nose. "The planogram is a proven formula to increase customer purchases."

"Yes, I vaguely remember you saying that before," Veronica said morosely, but her sarcasm went right over Lola's head.

"Miss? Excuse me?" Veronica turned around to see a thirtysomething woman who looked vaguely familiar standing there.

"May I help you?" Lola interjected, stepping in front of Veronica.

To Veronica's surprise, the woman motioned Lola to step aside. "I came to talk to her," she said, pointing at Veronica. "Or, more accurately, to thank her. You," she corrected, smiling at Veronica.

"Me?" Veronica asked.

The woman nodded. "I don't know if you remember me, but I was in here the other day. I tried on a strapless brown dress with a matching sweater."

Veronica nodded in recognition. "Oh, yes. I remember you. I told you that the dress made you look—oh, how did I describe it?"

"Like a stuffed sausage," the woman replied.

"Yes, that's right," Veronica said as Lola let out an audible gasp. "It's all coming back to me."

"I'm so sorry—," Lola began.

"I wanted to thank you for telling me that," the woman said, reaching out to clasp Veronica's hand. "I buy a lot of clothes in expensive stores, but no one has ever had the guts to tell me that something I liked didn't look good on me. You're the first salesperson to tell me the truth about how I looked. And you know what? You were right. That dress didn't make me look good."

Veronica blushed. "Maybe stuffed sausage was a little harsh."

"No, no, you were right," the woman

insisted. "It hurt my feelings, but you know, I think I needed that. I went home and thought about what you said about what would look good on me, and I came back today and found three dresses that really do work for my body type. And it's all because of you."

Tears sprung from Veronica's eyes as she impulsively reached out and hugged the woman. "Those dresses are perfect for you," she said, stepping back to look at them. "Please. Let me walk you to the cash register." A happy glow filled Veronica's heart. This is what fashion was all about—connecting customers with styles that work for them.

"Thanks again," the woman said once her purchases had been rung up and placed into a pink shopping bag. "I'll be back!" She looked over at Jane, then pointed to Veronica. "This girl is a keeper!"

Jane smiled. "She sure is." The manager gave Veronica a thumbs-up. "That was terrific, Veronica. You're exactly the type of employee Belle Pink needs."

"Why, thank you," Veronica said, thrilled.

She couldn't help herself: She gave Lola a smug smile.

"In fact, starting with your next shift, I want you front and center—working the floor." Jane clasped her hands together. "That's where you belong."

Veronica beamed.

She couldn't have agreed more.

Chapter 8

"Thanks, Mom," Betty said as her mom put a plate of steaming Belgian waffles and crispy bacon in front of her. "I really, really appreciate it." Her cat, Caramel, walked over and rubbed her back against Betty's leg. Betty reached down and gave the kitty an affectionate ear scratch.

Mrs. Cooper looked taken aback at her daughter's words. "You're welcome. I'm not used to such appreciation around here."

Betty sighed. "Now that I'm working at Pop's, any time someone brings *me* a plate of food, instead of the other way around, I'm happy." She dug in to her food, enjoying every bite.

Her mom sat down at the table. "You know, honey, Dad and I really appreciate how hard you're working this summer. And it's going to make your laptop mean that much more to you knowing that you earned the money for it yourself."

Betty chewed some waffle. "I know," she said after swallowing. "But I just wish I had more time to hang out with my friends."

"You're going to the beach later with Midge, right?"

Betty nodded. "It's all I'm thinking about."

Mrs. Cooper laughed and ruffled Betty's blond hair. "Make the most of your summer. Pretty soon you'll be like your sister, working all year long." Just then the phone rang. "Speaking of Polly, that should be her calling now. Love you, honey."

"Love you," Betty said as her mom clicked on the phone and walked into the family room. Her older sister, Polly, had moved to San Francisco a while ago, but she called her mom at least three times a week.

Betty took a sip of orange juice and picked

up the newspaper her dad had left on the table. She flipped to the horoscopes page and slid her finger down to her sign.

CANCER

Don't try to hold on to something if it's trying to get free. When one door closes, another always opens. Bright days are coming soon if you just hang in there and don't get caught up in others' small-mindedness.

"Bright days are coming," Betty said thoughtfully, putting the paper down. Maybe that meant a sunny day at the beach later today. She hopped up from the table and put her dishes in the dishwasher. "And as soon as I get through my shift at Pop's, the faster I can be there!"

XOXO

"You got it. Coming right up," Betty said, dashing back to the prep station. The orange coffeepot was getting dangerously near empty, so she took out the filter, popped a new one in, filled it with coffee grounds, poured in the water, and started brewing a new pot.

Betty wasn't sure how it had happened, but today had been the first day since she'd been working at Pop's that she felt on top of things. Her mom's words had stuck with her. She was right: Betty should be making the most of her summer. And by the end of it she'd have a nice pile of cash to spend on whatever she wanted.

Once the coffee was dripping into the pot, Betty headed back out to the restaurant where she refilled the empty straw dispensers in her station. "Hey, lady!" a little boy called. He was standing in front of the jukebox. "Do you know where I can get a quarter?" he asked. "I wanted to play a song."

Betty reached into her apron pocket and fished out two coins. She handed them to the little boy. "Make sure you pick a good one," she said, giving him a wink. And then she was off to her next table. She was so familiar with the menu now that when people ordered the Farmer's Omelet or the Handyman's

Hamburger, she didn't stare blankly at them. She knew exactly what they wanted.

The Chocklit Shoppe was beginning to fill up. Betty snuck a peek at her watch. She had finished the first hour on her shift without spilling a single drink—or breaking a dish. "One hour down . . . and only five left to go," she said to herself as she picked up the now-full coffeepot and began to pour refills for her customers. "What could go wrong?"

A family of four sat down at one of Betty's booths, and Betty soon discovered what could go wrong. In minutes, they had killed her good mood. They were loud, demanding, and kind of rude.

"Laptop. Laptop. Shiny keys. Big screen. Wi-Fi," she chanted under her breath as she made sure her customers' every desire was granted.

"Excuse me. Miss? Miss!" The mother was trying to get Betty's attention, waving her hand in an obnoxious manner.

Betty sighed. *What could be the problem now? I brought them ice water, more straws, another spoon, and their orders: four banana splits.*

"Yes?" Betty said, walking over. She was sure it was something totally urgent—like an extra napkin.

"Where I come from, banana splits usually have bananas in them," the mother snapped, shooting Betty the death glare.

Betty blinked. She stared down at the table. Four dishes of ice cream, chocolate sauce, whipped cream, and cherries stared back at her. There was not a banana in sight.

"Oh. My. Gosh. I'm so sorry!" she exclaimed. *How embarrassing!* She turned on her heels and ran over to the soda counter. "I need four bananas peeled pronto!" she instructed the guy working behind the soda fountain counter who was responsible for making Pop's delicious shakes, malts, sundaes . . . and banana splits. "And next time?" she said, giving the soda jerk a good-natured scolding. "Please try to remember that there are actual bananas in a banana split!"

XOXO

"Ooh la la, j'adore le jeans, ooh, ooh, j'adore le fashion," Veronica sang as she neatened up a rack of dresses. "La la la, *je suis une* fashion baby."

She buzzed over to a table and expertly folded two stacks of sweaters. Belle Pink always played the same playlist of songs, and by now Veronica knew them by heart. Most of the songs were either in French or had something to do with fashion, or in this case, both. They were always very catchy.

"That color would be fantastic with your skin tone," she chirped to a girl who was looking at a gold-colored shirt. Then Veronica wrinkled her nose as she passed by another customer. "Run as far away as possible from that scoop neck T-shirt. Totally not your style."

The girl gave Veronica a strange look. Veronica knew not everyone appreciated the advice, but it was for the greater good of fashion. She was definitely doing these customers a favor.

Ever since Jane had moved her to the

selling floor, Veronica had been in her element. And for every uptight person that got offended by one of Veronica's comments, there were at least three people who were happy to get the advice.

"I could totally see you work a Katy Perry vibe," she told another customer—a short girl with pigtails and a hand-painted knapsack. "We've got some tops and minidresses over here that you would be a knockout in. Bright colors that pop!"

"Really?" the girl said, eagerly going to where Veronica had pointed. Veronica watched, a satisfied smile on her face. The fashion business was just too much fun.

"Now how did this end up here?" Veronica said to herself, plucking a black satin tunic off a rack of sparkly tops. When she looked around to find the rack it belonged on, she noticed Liam across the mall. She waved hello. He pointed to his watch and lifted his hand up and down.

Veronica stared at him, puzzled for a second before it hit her: He was pretending to eat something . . . *He wants me to join him on his lunch break,* she realized, lighting up.

She caught his attention and held up her hand, her fingers spread out. "Five minutes," she mouthed, trying to remain calm, cool, and collected.

Suddenly her own lunch break had gotten a lot more interesting.

XOXO

"So where do you want to go?" Liam asked as they walked into the food court. The perimeter was lined with brightly colored fast-food restaurants while the middle was filled with tables and chairs.

"Oh, I don't care," Veronica said. And she really didn't. She was just happy to be hanging out with him. "I like most anything. Maybe the pizza place? Or the smoothie shop?"

Liam nodded. "Pizza sounds cool." They went over to the restaurant and ordered some slices and bottled waters. They each paid for their own lunch. *Of course he's not going to pay for me,* Veronica thought. *I mean, it's not like we're on a date or anything.* Sometimes that even got weird for Veronica. Because when she went out with boys who had a lot less money than she did, sometimes she felt guilty letting them pay for her. Her mother told her that it was completely fine—in fact, it was courteous for the boys to pay. Veronica was never quite sure what to do.

"I'm glad we can have lunch together," Liam said as they carried their food trays to an empty table. "I look for you every time I'm at work."

"You do?" Veronica asked, feeling a happy little shiver of excitement run up her spine. "I always look for you, too."

"That day you came in with your friend— you were two of the prettiest girls I've ever seen," Liam said as they sat down. "And, well, I wanted to make a good impression on you guys."

Veronica laughed. "We were, um, both kind of checking you out."

Liam's cheeks turned pink, whichVeronica found adorable. "Yeah . . . I kind of noticed."

"So," Veronica said, taking a dainty bite of her cheese pizza, "where do you go to school? Not Riverdale, right? That's where I go." Veronica knew everyone at Riverdale High, and she definitely would have noticed someone like Liam.

"I'm at Pembroke," Liam told her. "I moved here last year from Florida."

Veronica raised her eyebrows. She couldn't believe a nice guy like Liam went to stuck-up Pembroke Academy. Pembroke was a big rival of Riverdale's and tended to have a lot of snobby people. *But Liam is totally real and down-to-earth.*

"People have been pretty nice, but I'm still getting used to things, you know?" Liam said before taking a bite of his pizza. "And my classes are kind of tough. I couldn't believe how much homework we have."

"Tell me about it," Veronica agreed. Then she brightened. "But who wants to talk about boring stuff like that?" She reached over and pinched Liam's bicep. "You definitely are into sports, right? You look like you're the athletic type."

"I guess you could say that." Liam smiled

his crooked smile, making Veronica's heart swoon. "I'm on the football team. And basketball. You should come to a game sometime." Then Liam frowned. "Except Riverdale is one of our big rivals, so . . . maybe that wouldn't work out so well."

Veronica imagined herself in the stands at a football game, wearing a wool sweater and cute jeans, a soft plaid scarf around her neck, and her hair pulled up in a high ponytail as she stood and cheered for Liam as he ran for a touchdown. She was a great girlfriend—she loved supporting her boyfriends, cheering them on.

"Just because I go to Riverdale doesn't mean I can't be a fan of another team," she said coyly, looking at Liam through her thick eyelashes. Inside, though, she knew that Archie would be furious if he saw Veronica cheering for another boy . . . let alone one from posh Pembroke.

But a little jealousy could be good for a girl. And Liam was so cute and sweet. *It would be nice to go out with someone new . . . and it would probably be just a summer thing, anyway . . .*

"So, um, Veronica?" Liam asked, looking down at the table—and then suddenly straight into her eyes.

"Yes?" she said, feeling her heart skip a beat. His eyes were so warm . . . and his voice was so gentle and soft.

"I only get a half hour for lunch," he said apologetically. "I wish I could hang out with you longer." He crumpled up his napkin and tossed it on his tray.

"Me too," Veronica said, not wanting the moment to end. "I probably should be getting back to work."

Liam put the cap back on his water bottle. Then he took it off. Then he put it on again. "I was wondering if you might want to hang out at the beach tomorrow," he blurted out, looking at her with those warm brown eyes. "Together, I mean. That is, if you aren't working."

"Yes!" Veronica answered. "I mean, no, I'm not working. And yes, I'd love to hang out with you."

"Really?" Liam grinned. "Cool." He took

out his phone. "Let me have your number."

They exchanged contact info and cleared their trays.

Archie is definitely going to be jealous, Veronica thought, sneaking a peek at Liam's profile as they walked back to their stores. For that matter, so were Midge, Nancy, and Betty.

Because Veronica had the one thing that every girl wanted in the summertime.

The beginning of what could end up being a real summer love.

Chapter 9

Ever since Betty had been working at the Chocklit Shoppe, she had had a recurring nightmare: She did something horribly, embarrassingly wrong, and everyone in the restaurant stopped eating, forks held in midair, to stare at her in horror. Her "dream mistake" was never the same horrible, embarrassing thing. One night it was that she brought the wrong orders to an entire table of Pop's best customers. Another night she had worn a gorilla outfit to work. No matter what the cause, the effect was always the same—shocked, horrified stares combined with mocking laughter.

So when Betty went in through the out

door during her shift and skidded headfirst into Georgette, the result was exactly what Betty had been unintentionally preparing for since the day she started.

"Ahhhhhh," Betty cried, her sneakers squealing on the linoleum floor. The tray she had been holding flew up wildly in the air . . . and she went tumbling the other way.

Like a scene from a corny comedy movie, Betty found herself in a tangled heap on the floor with Georgette. Pieces of broken glass and smashed dinner plates surrounded them. A small dollop of pudding sat atop Georgette's bun.

"I'm so sorry," Betty managed to croak out, wiping some mashed potatoes off her cheek. "I—I don't know what happened."

"You went in the wrong door," Georgette said, her face wincing in a pained, pinched way. She waved to all the people who were staring at them. "Sorry about that, everyone. We're fine, we're fine."

"You don't look fine," Betty said, taking a big, steadying gulp of air. She gingerly stood up, trying not to cut herself on any of the broken glass.

"What was that?" Pop exclaimed, hurrying over. "Are you okay?"

"Besides being extremely mortified, I'm all right," Betty said, humiliated beyond words. She hadn't thought she could feel worse than she did in her recurring nightmares. Wrong, wrong, wrong!

Pop extended a hand to Georgette as a busboy started sweeping up the mess. People returned to their meals and conversations. "Watch yourself, Georgette."

But Georgette didn't move. "I think I sprained my ankle," she said, squeezing her eyes shut. "It really hurts."

Betty began gulping more air. "I am sooooo sorry," she said, her eyes filling with tears. How could she have been so klutzy?

Pop put his hands on her shoulders. "The show must go on, Betty. Can you handle Georgette's tables while we go get her ankle checked out? There's an urgent care clinic just down the road."

"Um, sure. Of course," Betty told him, wiping away a tear and pasting on the biggest *I'm fine!* smile she could muster.

Did she even have a choice?

XOXO

"Dude! You totally annihilated that guy," Reggie yelled, grinning over at Jughead. The two guys were standing in front of a huge flat-screen TV in Archie's basement.

Jughead blew on his knuckles. "What can I say? When you play this game for three hours straight every day, you better have some skills to show for it."

"You sure you don't want a turn, Betty?" Midge asked, dangling her remote control in front of Betty's face.

"No, Midge. Really, don't worry about it," Betty said, shaking her head. "I'm not really in the mood to play video games." It was her day off from work, but she wasn't actually much in the mood to do anything.

Betty sank deeper into the couch. Usually she had a good time hanging out with her friends in Archie's basement, watching movies and playing video games. But not today.

Veronica was supposed to join them, but at the last minute, she had texted Betty, telling her something came up and that she wasn't going to be able to make it.

She's probably doing something fun and summery, Betty thought, feeling sorry for herself. *She's sure not sitting in a basement after having the worst week of her entire life.*

Midge plopped down next to her on the couch. Midge wasn't in The Archies, but she'd come over to watch the band practice. Her heart-shaped face was scrunched up with concern. "Poor you. What exactly happened yesterday, Betty? Do you want to talk about it?"

Betty took a long, deep sigh. After she had left Pop's, she'd gone home and told her mom everything. Mrs. Cooper had made her a steaming mug of cocoa and listened empathetically to everything Betty had said.

"This is an opportunity in the making— not a disaster," her mom had told her.

But that was easier said than done. "Well,"

Betty began, looking at Midge, "I kind of caused this accident at Pop's."

Midge nodded. "Yeah. I heard about it."

"From who?" Betty hadn't noticed Archie or any of their friends in the restaurant.

Midge bit her lip. "I probably shouldn't tell you this. But . . . there's kind of a photo of you on the ground that's making the rounds."

"Making the rounds?" Betty said, her eyes widening in horror.

"Yeah. You have mashed potatoes on your cheek, and . . . well, whatever. But who cares?" Midge tried to laugh it off. "I mean, people will forget all about it in a few days . . . or weeks. Right?"

Betty swallowed. "Right," she said in the most unconvincing voice ever. "The other waitress, Georgette, injured her ankle. She got it checked out and learned she needs to stay off her feet for at least a week—probably more. Pop asked me if I can handle things until she comes back."

"That's awesome, Betty!" Jughead cried, tossing his remote control into the air and catching it. He hit pause and the scene on the TV screen froze.

"I didn't know you were listening to our conversation," Betty replied, wrapping her arms around her chest. Even though these were her closest friends, it was hard not to feel self-conscious.

Jughead grinned. "Once you start talking about restaurants and food, I just can't help myself. My eavesdropping tendencies take over."

"Pop must really trust you a lot," Kevin said. He was going through a big box of video games, looking for what to play next.

"And if you're the main waitress, Coop, all the tips will belong to you," Archie reminded her.

Betty knew her friends were only trying to cheer her up, but their words had the opposite effect. Thinking about work made her think about Georgette and Pop. She didn't want to let either of them down.

"Hey, Jughead?" she called, scrambling to sit up. "Hand me a control, would you? On second thought, I think I do want to play after all." Maybe running around a virtual forest carrying a slew of weapons in her back pocket as she chased nameless, faceless villains unleashing fatal strikes would help Betty get out all her negative energy.

Or maybe she'd end up being eaten by a fire-breathing dragon.

XOXO

Normally Veronica liked to be fashionably late and show up ten minutes after she was supposed to be somewhere. But she had been so excited to see Liam that she had left her house right on time. There hadn't been much traffic, and she had scored a parking spot in a beachfront lot. So that explained why she was standing alone on the boardwalk, trying to look cool as she waited for Liam to arrive.

This was totally worth spending my first paycheck on, she thought, looking down at her new halter top bikini with the gold foil circle print. So cute. If she needed to save her paychecks like Betty had to, she would be in big trouble. Her paychecks were more like fun money.

She pulled out her phone from her beach tote and looked at her messages.

8:34: Dad: Love you. Have a good weekend.

Her father was on business in Dallas.

9:03: Mom: Have fun 2day! Remember your sunscreen!

10:44: Reggie: At beach with Archie. Wanna hang out?

10:47: Midge: Movies? Us? Later?

The sound of the bus startled Veronica, and she looked up from her phone. The bus had just let out a group of passengers, and one of them was walking straight toward her.

Liam! Veronica waved, trying to ignore the ping-pong ball ricocheting around in her heart. She was kind of surprised that Liam had arrived on the bus. People from Pembroke weren't usually big on public transportation.

How cool is that, though? she thought as he got closer. He had on navy-blue swim trunks and a faded green T-shirt, and a backpack was slung over his shoulder. *He doesn't even care about what all those Pembroke snobs would think. Instead of driving, he's being extra green and eco-friendly.*

"Hey, you," he said, leaning over to kiss her on the cheek. "So this is where you hang out, huh?"

Veronica kissed his cheek back. He smelled like lemon and freshly cut grass, like maybe he'd just mowed the lawn and had a glass of lemonade before he came to the beach. "Yeah," she said, looking around as if she were seeing it for the first time. "It's a really nice beach. Come on, let's walk."

Liam reached out and took Veronica's hand. "I'm glad you can show it to me," he said, lacing his fingers with hers. "I've lived here for a while now, but there's so much stuff I haven't done yet."

"Allow me to be your personal tour guide then," Veronica said, resting her head on his shoulder for a second. "That section of the beach?" She pointed. "Very family-oriented. We hang out a little farther down. There's a little shop that sells sand toys and T-shirts, and next to that is the snack bar, which isn't too bad." Then Veronica pointed to a nondescript one-story building. "But that's the most important building of all."

"Lifeguard headquarters?" Liam asked.

Veronica shook her head. "Bathrooms."

As they approached the part of the beach where Veronica and her friends usually went, Veronica scanned the scene for her friends. It wasn't long before she spotted Archie's red hair and Reggie's broad shoulders. They were in the middle of playing catch.

"Do you want to find a place over here to put our stuff?" Liam asked.

Veronica nodded. "Sure!" They made their way down the wooden steps and began walking across the beach. "Ooh, it's so hot," Veronica said as the sand burned her feet.

"Want me to carry you?" Liam asked.

Veronica beamed at him. "Aww, how

chivalrous!" Giggling, she put her arms around Liam's neck, and he scooped her up in one fell swoop as if she was as light as a feather.

Out of the corner of her eye, she caught Reggie and Archie staring over at her, their mouths hanging open. There was no doubt about it: They looked totally shocked to see her with Liam.

She glanced their way and pretended to see them for the first time. "Oh, hi there," she called, waving to the boys. Then as Liam kept walking, she waved again. "Bye!"

1:30: Veronica: I love making boys jealous. LOVE IT.

1:32: Betty: Where r u?

1:33: Veronica: At beach with Liam! So FUN!

1:36: Betty: Having a bad day here. V. Bad.

1:36: Veronica: Why? What's up?

1:38: Betty: Can't tell you in a text. Call me 2night.

1:44: Veronica: OK. ttyl. Gotta run!

"Do you want to get ice cream?" Liam asked Veronica as they approached the snack shop. After lying on the beach for a while and cooling off in the surf, they had decided to take a walk along the boardwalk.

"Do you have to even ask?" she joked. "I've had my heart set on a mint chocolate chip cone from the moment we got here."

It had been such a fun day. Veronica had learned a lot about what Liam liked to do. Besides football and basketball, he also played tennis and lacrosse, and he had won a couple of mathematic competition awards. He was an only child, his favorite movie was *Gladiator*, and chirping crickets freaked him out. She also discovered that they were both country music fans—and that they each slept with a teddy bear! *We have so much in common*, Veronica thought happily as they got in line. It seemed like everyone was in the mood for ice cream.

She didn't think Liam realized who she was—that her father was *the* Hiram Lodge. And she liked it that way. That meant that Liam was interested in her for her and not because she was rich.

While they were waiting for their cones, Veronica spotted one of the biggest snobs around town: Bunny Smythe. Just seeing her made Veronica's blood boil. Bunny also went to Pembroke Academy and was one of the most horrible girls Veronica had ever met. She seemed to make it her personal mission to put down Riverdale High whenever she could. Today Bunny was wearing a tiny tie-dyed bikini and, as usual, was surrounded by her clique of mean girlfriends. They were just off the boardwalk in the middle of setting up their beach towels next to the lifeguard station.

That's typical Bunny, Veronica thought, rolling her eyes. The fact that the girls were positioned near the station was no accident.

Everything Bunny did was strategic. Veronica pitied the poor lifeguard, having to listen to them yapping the whole day.

Veronica knew it was childish, but she couldn't think of anything better than Bunny and her snobby friends seeing her with Liam. She loved the idea of rubbing her cute new guy in their stuck-up faces.

And like an answer to a prayer, Bunny and her friends simultaneously glanced their way. Just as Reggie's and Archie's had a few hours ago, the girls' mouths dropped open as their glances turned to stares.

Oh, yes. They are so totally jealous, Veronica thought gleefully, resisting the urge to laugh.

Instead, Veronica smiled brightly over at them as if they were all best friends. She pulled out her phone and sent Betty a quick text before tossing it back into her beach tote.

2:48: Love making mean girls jealous even MORE.

"Do you know those girls?" Liam asked, tilting his chin toward them. He licked his chocolate cone. "I think they might go to Pembroke. I've seen the blonde before. They're kind of staring at us."

And then Liam reached over and took her hand.

"They look kind of familiar," Veronica said, squinting at them in the sun as if she was trying to place them. "They have those plain, generic types of faces, you know?" Then she sighed happily. "This ice cream is so good it should be outlawed," she told him, taking a lick of her own mint chocolate chip. Veronica looked back over at Bunny and her friends.

The look on their plain, generic faces was priceless.

And so was the feeling of holding hands with the cutest boy on the boardwalk.

Chapter 10

"You don't understand," Betty said.

She had flopped onto her bed the moment she'd gotten home from work, not even bothering to change out of her clothes. "It was the worst day of my life. Georgette is hurt, and it's my fault, Pop hates me, and pretty soon all of Riverdale is going to see what a horrible waitress I am."

She squeezed her eyes shut, trying to block out the scene in the restaurant. Even though a few days had passed, it was like an endless loop in her mind—like a video clip on YouTube that no matter how many times she tried to hit pause continued to play. *Somebody probably did film it. It probably will end up on YouTube. The whole world will know how much I stink!*

"I'm sure it's not as bad as you think it is," Veronica said on the other end of the phone, her voice upbeat. "Besides, everyone makes mistakes."

Betty sniffled. She had been counting on Veronica for a little moral support, but Veronica was clearly having a much better week than she was. First, there had been all her text messages about Liam. He was so cute! So funny! So sweet! And the second Betty had heard Veronica's bubbly and breathless voice on the phone, she had regretted asking her to call in the first place. How could someone who was having such an awesome week sympathize with someone who was having such a terrible one?

She should have just suffered in silence.

"I just don't think I'm cut out to be a waitress," Betty said, feeling very sorry for herself. Caramel padded into the room and curled up next to Betty's slipper. Betty sighed. Life was so much easier for a cat.

Betty rolled over onto her stomach—then sniffed. Something smelled disgusting. To her horror, she realized it was her. "And eww! My hair smells like greasy french fries."

"You can't quit if that's what you're thinking," Veronica told her. "You have to stick it out for Georgette's and Pop's sakes. You owe them."

"Thanks for telling me something I didn't know," Betty mumbled. "That's what makes it even worse."

"Don't forget the reason you wanted a job this summer, Betty," Veronica reminded her. "Laptop?" Then Veronica let out a half giggle, half swoony sigh. "Laptops make me think of Liam. Betty, we had the best time today. Wait. Hold on. I'm going to send you a picture of us. Hang up and call me back after you see it."

A few seconds later Betty's phone buzzed in her hand. She clicked open Veronica's text. The happy new couple was standing on the boardwalk, heads together. Liam was laughing, and Veronica was making a silly face. They were holding dripping ice-cream cones.

Betty called Veronica back. "Yeah, I get it, okay? He is supercute."

There was a moment of silence. "Oh, Betty. You aren't mad at me, are you? I wasn't trying to make you feel bad. It's just hard not to be excited, and when I'm excited, you're the person I always want to share things with."

"I'm not mad," Betty said truthfully. "I'm happy that you're having such an awesome summer. I just wish that mine would perk up a little," she said wistfully.

"Did any of the other jobs you applied for work out? Did anyone else call you?" Veronica asked.

"No," Betty said, covering her face with her pillow.

"Well, see? You were meant to be a waitress," Veronica said. "Everything happens for a reason, Betty. There's a reason you got that job."

Veronica's words reminded Betty of her horoscope from that morning. *Luck will find you when you least expect it . . . but you have to be ready to receive it. So don't be shy. Get out there and shine, Cancer!* She *was* pretty lucky that she'd even gotten the waitressing job. Especially when she had had zero experience being a waitress. "I do like getting to meet new people," she said, her voice small. "That's been fun."

"See?" Veronica prompted. "Focus on the positive stuff."

"Pop hired me because I'm dependable and reliable," Betty said, half to herself.

"Absolutely."

"And I'm friendly, too."

"You are!"

A tiny pinpoint of brightness was beginning to light up Betty's world. "Thanks, Ronnie. For cheering me up."

"Anytime."

Betty said good night and clicked off the phone. Then she reached over to her nightstand, picked up her journal, and began to write.

> *When life hands you lemons, make*
> *lemonade! Everyone knows that*
> *old cliché. But clichés exist for a*

reason—they make a lot of sense!
Getting a summer job was all I could
think about. But when I got the job
at Pop's, it threw me a little because
it was completely out of my comfort
zone. I wasn't really sure I could be
a waitress . . . and to be honest, I'm
still not sure I can be. But I don't
really have a choice now. Someone is
hurt because of me, and as much as
I wish I could, I can't turn around
and change things. The only thing I
can do is try not to be a wimp and do
the very best job I can. If I suck . . . I
suck! It's not like I'm filling in for a
brain surgeon . . . or a World Series
pitcher . . . or a chef at a five-star
restaurant.

I'm a waitress at a diner for
Pete's sake. If people are going
to judge me, well . . . that's their
problem.

Working at Pop's Chocklit
Shoppe was not my dream job, but it

sure is teaching me a lot. And that's
the important thing. (Okay, making
$$$$$ is also pretty important!!)

Betty tucked her pen inside the journal and smiled. Putting her thoughts on paper made her feel a lot better.

And she knew something else that would make her feel better: a long, hot bath.

XOXO

"*Merci!* Hope we see you again real soon," Veronica said, handing a large shopping bag to her latest customer. She hummed along to the song that was currently blasting through the Belle Pink speakers.

Work was going great—she was busy and having fun—and things with Liam were just as perfect. Tonight she was meeting him for pizza, and then they were going to rent a paddleboat on the lake.

So fun.

"Here you go," Veronica said now, putting a new customer's top into a bag. "Don't forget to check your e-mail for our special offers!"

She tucked in a sheet of bright pink tissue paper and fluffed it out. That was the last sheet of paper. Veronica walked to the back room to grab another box of the store's signature wrap before another customer could come up to pay.

The muffled sounds of crying greeted her when she pushed the door open. "Lola?" Veronica said hesitantly, her eyes widening in surprise. Her coworker was hunched over the table, her hair shielding her face. "What's wrong? Are you sick or something?"

Lola looked up at her. Her face was red and blotchy. She reached for a napkin someone had left behind on the table and loudly blew her nose. "I—I never thought you'd be so good at this job," she blurted out.

Veronica stared at her, trying to make sense of what was going on. "That's why you're crying?"

Lola hiccuped. "I underestimated you. You came in here looking all hip and cute and I—I'm just so boring next to you. No one asks my opinion about buying something. They just go straight to you, and you get credit for the sale."

"I'm sorry. I didn't mean for you to feel that way," Veronica said, biting her lip. "I'm just being myself."

Lola kept going. "And don't think I don't know that you roll your eyes at me when I follow the rules, but I can't help it. I'm a rule follower." She took a deep breath. "And then when I found out who your father is, I guess I thought that you would feel like you didn't have to work hard. That you could coast by."

Veronica wasn't surprised that Lola thought that way. Most people did. But because her father was a billionaire, she had to work twice as hard as anyone else in order to prove herself.

"And you aren't coasting by," Lola said. "You're working really hard, and you're doing a great job. So great that before long I'll probably be reporting to you."

"Don't be crazy," Veronica told her. "Jane loves you."

Lola didn't look convinced. "I haven't

been on the sales floor in days—and when I am, I barely rack up any sales. At this rate, I might even be fired."

Veronica walked over and pulled up a chair beside her coworker. "Lola, Jane is not going to fire you. You're an incredible employee. You just need to lighten up a little . . . and find your inner fashionista. I know she's in there somewhere." She reached for Lola's hand and pulled her to her feet. "Now go splash some cold water on your face and then let's go get to work."

"Why are you doing this for me?" Lola asked, not looking entirely convinced that this was a good idea.

Veronica flashed her a smile. "Because at Belle Pink it's important that we help our friends."

Chapter 11

Betty tried to keep a positive attitude the following week at the Chocklit Shoppe. And her friends and family had tried to be encouraging.

Dad: Keep your chin up, Betty. This is what separates the men from the boys.

Archie: It'll all be worth it when you get your laptop.

Polly: Pop is so sweet. Tell him I said hi!

Veronica: The waitress uniform is so cute on you!

Jughead: Are you kidding? It's the best job ever—all-you-can-eat free food!

But Betty had to admit it: Instead of getting better at waitressing, she was getting worse. She couldn't keep up with all the tables, and things were going from bad to awful. Her shifts were spent in a tizzy trying to keep up with the orders. A typical day went something like this:

Table Number One

Betty: "Hi! Can I take your order?"

Annoyed Customer Number One: "Um, we already ate. We're waiting for our check."

Betty: "Oops! Sorry!"

Table Number Two

Betty: "Here you go, sir. Pot roast and mashed potatoes."

Annoyed Customer Number Two: "That smells good. But I ordered the chicken potpie."

Betty: "Ohhhh. I think I gave that to the woman over there. I'll be right back."

Table Number Three

Betty: "Here's your check. Let me know if I can get you anything else."

Annoyed Customer Number Three: "How about our food?"

Pop pulled Betty off to the side of the restaurant. The lunchtime rush had subsided and just a handful of tables were left to take care of.

"Things got a little crazy out there today, Betty," Pop said, shaking his head. "We had some pretty unhappy customers."

"I am *so* sorry," Betty told him, apologizing for what felt like the hundredth time. "I'm trying to do a good job for you. I really am!"

"I've had to comp four tables' food today," Pop said, exasperated. "This is my business, Betty. I can't keep giving food away for free—but I have no choice if I want to make my unhappy customers leave satisfied."

Betty felt awful. At least he wasn't yelling at her—even though he probably felt like it.

"And I can't keep mopping up your messes," he went on, looking distracted. "I'm in the middle of updating the menu—adding some new items, changing some prices— and I've got to make my changes so I can get it printed before the deadline next month."

Just then the restaurant door opened and in walked Georgette. Or rather, she hobbled. She was on crutches. Seeing her only made Betty feel worse—if that was even possible.

Georgette made her way over to them. "I was in the neighborhood and thought I'd drop by to see how things are without me." She winked at Betty. "Keeping the place running for me?"

Betty tried to put on a brave face despite the sinking feeling in her stomach. "When do you think you'll be back at work?" It wouldn't be a moment too soon.

Georgette sighed. "Don't know yet. The doctor wants me to stay on crutches for a little longer."

Betty noticed a customer trying to get her attention. He was pointing at his plate and frowning. "Um, I better go. It was good to see you, Georgette. I hope your ankle gets better really soon."

"Hang in there, kid," Georgette said. "Soon you'll be working the room like a pro."

Betty managed a tiny smile, and then hurried off to face her latest annoyed customer. Soon couldn't come fast enough.

XOXO

Dusk was beginning to fall as Veronica and Liam walked out of the Riverdale movie theater holding hands. They'd caught the seven o'clock showing of *Big Bad Dream*—the third movie they'd seen together in the past two weeks.

Veronica didn't even really like horror movies, but they are filled with scary scenes that force you to hold hands with your guy. Sometimes you even have to bury your face in his neck. But she didn't much care what they saw as long as they got to spend some time together.

There was a slight chill to the summer night air, and Veronica was glad she'd brought a sweater with her.

"That was so awesome," Liam said animatedly as they strolled down the sidewalk past storefronts that were closed for the night. "When that freaky girl popped out of the water when those guys were on the dock and chased them with that buoy? Brilliant."

"I think I missed that part," Veronica said. She had kept her eyes closed through most of the movie.

"Aw, man, you did? Well, what about when the zombie kid was standing in the dark hallway outside his bedroom, and his parents thought he needed a glass of water, but he was out to kill them! That was crazy!"

"I missed that, too," Veronica said, shrugging.

Liam laughed. "Anyone ever tell you that you have superhuman strength? You were squeezing my hand so hard I thought you might have crushed my fingers. Did you see *any* of the movie?"

They waited for the light to turn red, then crossed the street. "Sure, I saw it," Veronica said. "I liked the part where the girls were having a sleepover and baked chocolate chip cookies."

Liam gave her an incredulous stare. "Veronica. That was a preview for another movie."

She shrugged again. "Well, I thought that it looked fun," she said with a sniff.

Liam let go of her hand to rub her arm. "You should have told me you weren't into horror movies. We could have gone to see something else."

Veronica nestled her head on his shoulder. He was just the right height—tall enough that her head fit comfortably but not so tall that she felt like she was with an NBA player. "It's okay. I didn't mind. Besides, I think we've seen all the other good ones." Veronica smiled to herself. Clearly Liam didn't know her theory that scary movies were the perfect kind of movie to go to with someone you liked: They gave you the perfect opportunity to hold hands and snuggle close with your guy.

And now they were doing something she loved to do after a movie—hanging out and talking.

Liam held the door to the Chocklit Shoppe open for her, and they walked inside. *Such a gentleman,* Veronica thought, glancing around the restaurant. She hoped there were people that she knew there to witness her date.

"So you pick the movie next time," he said as they sat down at a booth. "I'll even sit through a sappy romance if that's what you like."

What Veronica liked was that Liam was already talking about their "next movie" as if it was already understood that they'd be going on another date together.

"Do I look like a girl who would like a sappy romance?" she asked, looking at Liam.

She twirled a lock of her dark hair around her finger.

He looked back at her. "Uh . . . yeah. You look exactly like that."

Veronica giggled. Betty came over and handed them menus.

"Liam, this is my best friend in the world," Veronica said, smiling up at Betty. "Betty Cooper. And she's heard all about you. I'm so glad you guys can finally meet each other!"

"Really?" Liam said. "I hope it was all good stuff."

Betty laughed. "Now what fun would that be? I'll be back in a minute to take your order," she told them before hurrying over to another table.

"Poor Betty," Veronica said under her breath. "She's been working so hard here. And it's especially brutal because she has to deal with all sorts of customers, and some of them are really mean and rude."

Speaking of which, Veronica had just noticed Bunny and her mean girl clique sitting a few tables behind Liam. They were huddled over ice-cream sodas, and Veronica was certain they had noticed her and Liam. And then she caught Bunny staring over at them. *Yes, we are still together,* she thought smugly, remembering the day at the beach.

Might as well give them something new to talk about, Veronica decided. She reached across the table to hold Liam's hands. "So are you working tomorrow? I was thinking that maybe we could have a picnic in the park."

"I get off work at five. We could make it a picnic dinner," Liam suggested. "There's a summer jazz concert series going on. We could hang out and eat and catch the tunes."

Veronica couldn't think of anything more romantic than sitting with Liam on a plaid wool blanket, with a wicker picnic basket filled with gourmet cheeses, grapes, and crusty bread, and some cool jazz music drifting through the summer nighttime sky. *We can feed each other grapes and wrap our arms around each other, counting stars . . .*

Just then Betty came over to take their

orders, breaking up Veronica's romantic daydream.

"How about a big hot fudge sundae with two spoons?" Liam suggested, looking over at Veronica.

"Yum. Sign me up," she said happily.

"He's a keeper. So cute," Betty mouthed to her, giving her a thumbs-up behind Liam's back before hustling off to the kitchen to put in the order.

Veronica looked over at him. He was pretty adorable. She felt like putting her hand in his shaggy hair and mussing it up, but decided that would not be a very cool thing to do. Then she remembered what Liam had been talking about. "That picnic and concert sound cool," Veronica told Liam. "When do you want to pick me up?"

Liam paused. "I'm, uh, not sure. Let me find out if, uh, my dad needs his car."

"Okay," Veronica said. "Or I can pick you up if you need me to." Veronica hadn't been to Liam's house yet, and she was dying to get a peek. She wanted to learn everything she could about her new boyfriend. Seeing where he lived would be another cool part of the Liam puzzle.

Could she call him her boyfriend? He was definitely acting like a boyfriend—holding her hand, holding open the door, paying for her movie ticket, making plans to hang out again . . .

I can definitely call him my boyfriend, she decided, sneaking a glance over at Bunny. She was blabbing away to her friends, covering her mouth with her hand, and making her eyes wide in her typical drama queen way.

"Hey, before our food comes, I'll be, uh, right back," Liam said, leaning over to give her a kiss.

Veronica felt a little surge of electricity from her lips all the way down to her toes.

"Okay," she said, watching as he stood up and headed toward the restrooms.

She'd never felt this way about a boy—not with Archie, not with Reggie, and not with any of the other ones she'd gone out with.

What did it mean? Was she ready to

settle down with someone? She almost couldn't believe it. *And to think that he's not even a student at Riverdale!* Dating someone from another school was definitely going to have some ups and downs. It was okay for now, while it was summer, but once fall rolled around and school started up again, it was going to be difficult to make sure they saw each other.

I guess I'll just cross that bridge when I come to it, she decided blissfully, taking a sip of water. For now she was just going to enjoy the ride.

She was startled back to reality when Bunny and her friends sauntered over.

Veronica frowned. They were definitely up to no good.

"So, Veronica, enjoying your job this summer?" Bunny asked, putting her hand on her hip. Bunny's two friends stood on either side of her, wearing virtually identical jeans and T-shirts. Their long hair swished in tandem. They were the stereotypical mean girl sidekicks.

"It's so nice of you to ask," Veronica said, oozing charm and putting on a big smile. "It's been fantastic. Not only do I get to see the latest fashions first, but I'm getting amazing experience for my college applications."

Bunny let out a surprised gasp. "Oh, wow. I didn't know you were going to be a preschool teacher." She turned to her friends. "Isn't that admirable? Someone with all that Lodge family money deciding to enter such a noble profession."

Veronica was really confused. "I'm not going to be a teacher. I'm working at Belle Pink. The clothing store at the mall?" She wasn't sure what Bunny was up to, but she was starting to get a bad feeling.

The sidekicks giggled, sounding like laughing hyenas. "Aren't you babysitting this summer?" one of them asked, pursing her lips, her eyes flitting over Veronica.

"Yeah," said the other girl. She snapped her bubble gum. "Because if you aren't, then why else would you be hanging out with a boy *two years younger* than you are?" The girl said the words *two years younger* in a very slow, drawn-out way.

Veronica let out a gasp. "What?" she blurted out before she could stop herself. She tried to make sense of what they were telling her. Was Liam—her sweet, cute, funny, nice new boyfriend—really two years younger than she was?

Dating a younger boy was a huge no-no for Veronica. It just wasn't cool for someone of her stature at Riverdale High to do. An incoming senior dating a sophomore? It made Veronica almost lose her lunch. And Bunny and her friends knew it.

"Cradle rob much?" Bunny cackled. She turned to her friends, and they all cracked up. "See?" Bunny said gleefully. "I told you guys. She had no clue she was going out with such a baby."

Veronica's blood was churning inside her. She was so horrified that she didn't even care if Bunny and her friends saw how upset she was. She yanked her purse from the seat next to her, then stood up and brushed past the mean girls. When she reached the front of the restaurant, she took out her phone and began typing a text to Liam, her fingers punching the buttons in a frenzy.

MEET ME OUTSIDE. NOW!!!!

Chapter 12

When you had been friends with someone as long as Betty had been best friends with Veronica, you had a pretty good idea when something was wrong. And by the scene Betty had just witnessed in the Chocklit Shoppe—Veronica storming out, then texting furiously, Bunny Smythe and her friends cracking up, and Liam walking out of the men's room to a deserted table, looking totally confused as he checked his phone—something was definitely up.

Betty looked at the clock. One hour left until her shift was finished and she could find out what was going on between Veronica and Liam.

She was in the middle of trying to spy on them through one of the fogged-up Chocklit Shoppe windows when she felt a tap on her shoulder.

"No luck. I can't see a thing," she said as she turned around, expecting to see Mikey, the cook. He loved getting caught up in drama.

But it wasn't Mikey. It was Pop.

"Can you come sit with me for a minute, Betty?" Pop asked, motioning to an empty booth. "I, uh, want to talk to you about something."

"Um, sure," she said, following him over. *I wonder what he wants to talk about,* she thought, feeling slightly nervous. Tonight had been a pretty decent night in her waitressing career—she'd only messed up two orders. She sat down in the booth across from Pop and folded her hands on the table.

"Okay, Betty. You're a good kid, and so I'm going to give it to you straight," Pop said, wiping some invisible sweat off his forehead. "I know you're trying your best, but by spilling food, breaking dishes, and upsetting my customers, having you work for me is costing me more money than you bring in."

Betty looked down, feeling terrible.

"Georgette will be back soon—and her twin sister, Lynette, is an experienced waitress and has offered to step in until she's back," Pop went on. "But it's not like I don't realize how hard you've been working, Betty, and I know how hard you've tried. So I'm willing to pay you for two more weeks of shifts . . . but you have to promise me you won't show up to work them."

Betty swallowed. "So you're saying you'd pay me . . . not to work?"

Pop nodded. "It's my cheapest option."

The idea of getting paid not to work sounded kind of appealing . . . but it really wasn't the outcome she was hoping for. "That's awfully kind of you, Pop," she said slowly. "I have to admit that being a waitress isn't really for me. But . . . I don't really think it would be right for you to pay me if I'm not working."

Pop patted her hand with his warm, fat fingers. "Like I said, Betty. You're a good kid. You sit here and think about it, all right? I'll handle the rest of the tables tonight."

Most of the restaurant had emptied out now. Betty was thankful that Bunny and her friends had already paid their check and left— she definitely didn't need them witnessing her humiliation.

She wasn't sure what to do. She definitely needed the money . . . but taking money for a job she wasn't doing felt wrong. She stared off into space. Without thinking, she picked up one of the Chocklit Shoppe's menus and opened it, then closed it. Opened it. Closed it. Opened it.

All of a sudden, an idea rushed into Betty's brain. An absolutely awesome idea.

There was something she could do for Pop to show how appreciative she was that he took a chance on her—and that he was being so generous.

I might be a terrible waitress . . . but I am a great writer, she thought excitedly, clicking open her pen. *And I know what customers want.*

Pop's tasty food wasn't going to change . . . but the way he presented it could definitely use an update.

She started on the left side. Appetizers. "Now, in a *regular* restaurant you could order french fries, but at Pop's Chocklit Shoppe, food is *lovingly prepared.* Here, you get to order *golden-brown* french fries. And cheese sticks? I think *deep-fried mozzarella served with a side of Pop's homemade marinara sauce* definitely has a better ring to it," she said to herself, writing on the menu. Inspiration flowed through her bones as she jotted down one idea after the next. "Boneless chicken strips would sound a lot better if they were *spicy* boneless chicken strips *served with blue cheese dressing.* And who wants a boring old chocolate milkshake when you can get a *death-by-chocolate* one?"

Tuning out everything around her, Betty spent the next hour editing and rewriting Pop's menu, making everything sound delicious. She added new categories, like

"Family Favorites" and "Create Your Own Sandwich."

She might not have earned her keep as a waitress. But Betty Cooper was going to make sure that she earned each and every penny Pop paid her.

XOXO

"How could you?" Veronica cried, folding her arms across her chest. "How could you lie to me about how old you are?" Veronica felt sick to her stomach. She should have known her summer romance was too good to be true. Talk about enjoying the ride! Veronica felt as if she'd just been pushed in front of a double-decker bus.

Liam hung his head. He'd barely said a word since they'd walked outside and over to a couple of swings in the park across the street. "Well, um, to be honest—"

"Yeah, that would be a good place to start," Veronica cut in angrily. She sat down hard on a swing and began to move slowly back and forth.

"I, um, never actually told you how old

I am," he said, shoving his hands in his pockets. He sat down on the swing beside her, tapping his toe rapidly and showing his nerves.

Veronica thought for a moment. It was true that she couldn't remember a specific moment when he told her his age—and she couldn't recall having asked him his age, either. *But why would I have?* she thought, shaking her head in frustration. If a boy asked her out, it was a given that he needed to be her age or a little bit older.

Apparently it was not a given to Liam.

"I thought if an older, beautiful, sophisticated girl like you knew I was only a sophomore, you'd never stoop to hanging out with me," he said softly, his voice cracking.

"Well, you thought right," she said sharply, not wanting to give him an inch.

"Come on, Veronica," Liam said, reaching out for her hand.

She pulled away, feeling dangerously close to tears. The seat of her swing banged into his.

"I'm still the same guy you were totally

into a few minutes ago. I mean, I get up to go to the men's room, and I come back and it's like you totally hate me."

Now the tears were welling up in her eyes.

"We've had so much fun this summer. Haven't we?" he asked, moving his swing around so he could stare into her eyes. "So I'm younger than you. So what? Age is just a number, isn't it?"

For several minutes, neither of them said anything. Veronica looked away, first out at the fringe of trees that surrounded the park and then up to the dark sky. It was filled with twinkling stars.

If she really thought about it, going out with a younger boy wasn't the end of the world. Sure, people like Bunny and her friends would think she was a total loser for doing it, but she didn't really care what those girls thought.

Veronica had always thought older boys were more mature. But Liam had seemed perfectly mature the whole time they'd been together. And the fact that he knew he was younger—and still tried to be with her—proved that he didn't really care what other people thought, either. He was brave enough to follow his heart.

Veronica turned to face him. "We did have a lot of fun together," Veronica said grudgingly, trying not to get sucked in by his hazel eyes, which looked even warmer and safer than ever. "And I guess I can't really blame you for wanting to hang out with a classy high-school girl. But . . . I can't help it. I like to go out with boys who have their driver's license." She gasped. "That's why you take the bus and haven't been able to pick me up, isn't it? You aren't old enough to drive yet!"

Liam gave her a sheepish shrug. "Yeah . . . but I do shave. That's something, isn't it?" he said, attempting to make a joke.

Veronica let out a laugh. "You're really funny. And sweet." Then she sighed. She knew that just because a boy was a senior and had a fancy car didn't necessarily mean he was mature or responsible. But for her, age wasn't just a number. She wished she could be cool with dating a sophomore, but she just couldn't be.

Maybe she was the immature one.

"The thing is, Liam, we both knew that this . . . this thing we have, whatever you want to call it—it was just a summer fling, anyway," Veronica told him, her heart heavy.

"It doesn't have to be," Liam said, reaching over to take her hand. His hands felt warm and strong, and she fought the urge to bury her head in his chest. "You said yourself that even though it would be a challenge to stay together once school started that it wouldn't be impossible."

"That was when I thought you were a senior," she said sadly. "But the reality is I have my real life back at Riverdale High, and you have yours back at Pembroke Academy." She decided it would be best to leave her on-again, off-again relationships with Archie and Reggie out of the equation. "Summer romance doesn't usually last once fall comes around, Liam."

Liam pulled Veronica close, and this time she didn't resist. "This has been one of the best summers of my life," he whispered, touching his nose to hers. "I'll never forget you."

"Me neither," Veronica whispered back. She and Liam had had some incredible conversations. They'd shared a lot these past few weeks. Maybe it had been easier to open up to him knowing in some part of her brain that it wasn't going to be forever.

Liam kissed her, and it was the sweetest kiss Veronica had ever had. She hugged him, breathing in the scent of shampoo in his hair and cologne on his neck. Then, she let her swing take her back, slowly pumping her legs to move herself forward.

"So was that a good-bye kiss?" Liam asked, drawing his eyebrows together. "Because that definitely felt like a good-bye hug."

"Hmmm. Let's call it a 'let's get together next summer and see where we are' kiss," she said, standing up. She felt sad, too. Deep in her heart, she'd known this moment was coming from the moment she'd first started a summer romance . . . she just hadn't anticipated it happening tonight.

"Come on," she told him, taking him by the hand. "Let's go home. And, um, Liam? I'll drive."

Chapter 13

"Look! No hands!" Veronica yelled, letting go of her mountain bike's handlebars as she and Betty coasted down a small incline in the park.

Veronica's long dark hair blew out behind her. It was a picture-perfect day: bright sunshine, cool breeze, no clouds. And it was made even sweeter by the fact that the two best friends were free again.

"Ronnie, you're crazy," Betty said, laughing. "But that's why I love you." She slid out her steel water bottle from her bike's holder and took a long, ice-cold gulp. "You better watch out, though, or you could end up with a broken arm."

"But then maybe I'd get a cute, young doctor to fix it," Veronica joked, batting her eyelashes. She took hold of the handlebars again and slowed so that Betty could pedal up to ride alongside her.

"I feel like the weight of the world has been lifted off my shoulders," Betty told Veronica. And she really did. "I am totally appreciating being a customer at Pop's again instead of being an employee."

Looking back on the past few weeks, Betty had to admit that the experience hadn't been all bad. She had learned a lot about the service industry—and that waitresses deserve every single tip they receive.

"I bet you'll be a big tipper from now on, right?" Veronica asked.

"Definitely," Betty said. "And I'm so glad that things are back to normal at the Chocklit Shoppe." Sam's had reopened the previous week, so the crowds at Pop's had eased up. Georgette's ankle was almost entirely healed— and her sister, Lynette, enjoyed the job and getting to work with her sister so much that she decided to become a full-time waitress at the restaurant.

"Things really couldn't have worked out any better. Pop just got in his new menus, and all my edits and changes are making a big difference," Betty said excitedly. "He said appetizer orders are through the roof!"

"Madame Veroniska sees a Pulitzer Prize for journalism in your future, Betty," Veronica teased.

Betty shrugged modestly. "It's just like my horoscope said today: 'With a little effort, you can accomplish anything you set your mind to.'" Then she laughed. "Pop wants me to write all his ad copy from now on . . . if I win the Pulitzer, my rate is going way up!"

The girls biked over a small footbridge and rounded a bend in the bike path. For a few minutes, neither of them talked, instead just enjoying the moment.

"It was a pretty difficult decision, but I really didn't have a choice," Veronica said, sounding wistful. "I had to quit working at Belle Pink. I mean, I loved my time there, but working . . . well, it just kept me away from all the things that are important to me. All our friends, playing keyboard with The Archies . . ."

"Sleeping in," Betty chimed in.

"That's the biggest thing." Veronica yawned. "I mean, they really should consider employees' sleep needs. Who decided ten o'clock was a good time to open up a store?"

"So have you heard from Lola?" Betty asked. Veronica had filled her in on Belle Pink's über employee, and she was curious to see how the girl was doing.

"She just texted me yesterday," Veronica said. "Honestly, I felt so proud of her. She told me that she created a new display at the front of the store that was entirely her idea—and that people have been buying the stuff she featured in it like crazy."

"We should go check it out," Betty said as they pedaled around an overgrown bush.

"Definitely."

The girls rode up to a huge maple tree and got off their bikes for an energy bar and water break.

"So if we go to the mall and walk into Belle Pink and Liam is working across the way . . . ," Betty began slowly, not sure how her friend would react.

"No problemo," Veronica said, giving a simple shrug. She leaned up against the tree, fanning herself with her hand. "I'm a big girl. I can handle it. We've even texted each other a couple times since we broke up. It's cool. I mean, it wouldn't have been fun to have to see him every day once we weren't with each other, but I've thought a lot about it, and really, what we had together was never going to be more than a summer fling."

Part of Betty wished that Veronica had kept her relationship going with Liam because then she wouldn't be competition for Betty back at school. Betty had a feeling that things at Riverdale High this year would be just like they always were—she and Veronica were the best of friends and total rivals when it came to boys, especially Archie. People had a hard time understanding how the two girls could remain such good friends when they were constantly competing for Archie's—and occasionally Reggie's—heart.

It didn't really make sense . . . but it was just one of those things, Betty thought, resigned to whatever happened. Boys could come and go, but a best friend was forever. She couldn't imagine being at Riverdale High without Veronica by her side.

"And don't forget, there's one thing about my summer romance that was pretty awesome." Veronica winked at Betty, and Betty laughed, knowing what she was alluding to.

"My laptop!" Betty hadn't managed to earn quite enough money for a laptop—but with the discount Veronica talked Liam into giving her, she was going to be able to afford a really nice one. "That was really sweet of him to give me the discount," Betty said. "He's a nice guy."

"Yeah," Veronica said, taking a crunchy bite of her energy bar. "Who knows? Maybe when he gets his driver's license I'll decide to go out with him again. But he'd have to have a pretty sweet car." Then she laughed.

"Kidding!" It was pure Veronica.

Betty knew there was a kernel of truth in what her best friend said. Veronica liked boys with lots of money and expensive sports cars. And she wasn't always easy to get along with. Liam probably got off easy.

Betty stretched her arms over her head and straddled her bike. "Ready?" she asked.

Veronica nodded, throwing her wrapper into a nearby trash can. "I've got a great idea," she said. "Why don't we bike over to my house and give each other manicures? I just picked up some new polish at the drugstore yesterday. There's this gorgeous rose color that would look so pretty with your skin tone."

Betty thought back to that day at the beginning of the summer when she and Veronica had passed by Beauty Town. It seemed like a lifetime ago. "That sounds awesome. Let me just text my mom so she knows where I am." She shot Veronica a quizzical glance. "But I'm surprised you want to do your own nails, spa girl. What's up with that?"

Veronica hopped back on her bike and

began to pedal down the path. "Betty, you should know this more than anyone," she called over her shoulder as Betty followed on her own bike. "After the summer we've had, spending twenty bucks on a manicure would be crazy. Because we've definitely learned the value of a dollar!"

Betty smiled. She wasn't sure saving money was a lesson privileged Veronica would remember for long. But there were a lot of things about that summer that would stay in both their memories—hard work, good friends, some laughs, a little romance . . .

And what lay ahead for them back at Riverdale High? Just like Betty's horoscope . . . it was written in the stars.